THE GAME

ALSO BY LINSEY MILLER

MASK OF SHADOWS

Mask of Shadows

Ruin of Stars

● ●

Belle Révolte

THE GAME

LINSEY MILLER

Underlined

All rights reserved. Published in the United States by Underlined, an imprint of
Random House Children's Books, a division of Penguin Random House LLC, New York.

Underlined is a registered trademark and the colophon
is a trademark of Penguin Random House LLC.

Visit us on the Web! GetUnderlined.com

Educators and librarians, for a variety of teaching tools,
visit us at RHTeachersLibrarians.com

Library of Congress Cataloging-in-Publication Data
Names: Miller, Linsey, author.
Title: The game / Linsey Miller.
Description: First edition. | New York : Underlined, 2020. | Audience: Ages 12 and up. |
Summary: "Every year the senior class at Lincoln High plays assassin. But this year,
the game isn't any fun—it's real."— Provided by publisher.
Identifiers: LCCN 2020009763 (print) | LCCN 2020009764 (ebook) |
ISBN 978-0-593-17978-9 (trade paperback) | ISBN 978-0-593-17979-6 (ebook)
Subjects: CYAC: Murder—Fiction. | Games—Fiction. | High schools—Fiction. |
Schools—Fiction.
Classification: LCC PZ7.1.M582 Gam 2020 (print) | LCC PZ7.1.M582 (ebook) |
DDC [Fic]—dc23

The text of this book is set in 11.5-point Adobe Garamond.
Interior design by Ken Crossland

Printed in the United States of America
10 9 8 7 6 5 4
First Edition

For my mother.

Thank you for introducing me to

the mystery section of the library.

CHAPTER 1

TO: 9781579126247@gmail.com
SUBJECT: The Game Begins
I am ready to kill or be killed. This email serves as the official notice that I, [NAME HERE], am entering this year's round of Assassins. I understand that I must send this email before midnight Wednesday and that I will receive the rules, my team members' names, and my target's name Friday at 12:00 p.m.
The game begins Friday at 5:00 p.m.
Wish me luck,
[NAME HERE]

"This is it," Lia said. She added her name to the email and read it over one last time. "Think we'll be the first?"

"I didn't wake up at five to not be." Gem launched themself off the bathroom counter and peered over Lia's shoulder. "It's simpler than I thought it would be."

"Dramatic, though." Lia nudged Gem in the side. "Do yours. We'll send them together."

1

Every March, in the anxiety-ridden weeks before colleges sent out acceptance decisions, the seniors of Lincoln High went to war. The game was the last great equalizer before the seniors went their separate ways.

And Lia—who had been planning her Assassins strategy since ninth grade, who had color-coded it red in her planner, and who had never been the best at anything—had already hung on her closet door a practical pair of running shoes, a black T-shirt she only mostly cared about, and a pair of leggings that wouldn't feel like sandpaper if they got wet.

Not that they would. She just liked to be prepared.

"Gem Hastings reporting for murder." Gem took a step back and raised their phone.

This year, the invitation to play was taped to the back of the bathroom doors. Few teachers ever ventured into these bathrooms, and even if one did, every bathroom was the same. Powder soap dusted the damp counters and inspirational posters decorated the dented stall doors. The invitation was a large poster of the white Lincoln High lion overlaid with three concentric circles in blood red. At their center was a QR code.

Assassins wasn't a school-approved event, but it was tradition. Anyone who wanted to play would know what this poster meant.

"Scanned," Gem said. The email opened, and they filled it out. "Three."

"Two," Lia said, thumb hovering over the SEND button.

It was only a game, but it was *the* game. It was hunting season for seniors. It was permission to stay out late with friends and teammates. It was the last chance for Lia to be good at something instead of being stuck in the shadow of her older brother.

"One," they both said.

The emails sent.

"I hope we're on the same team," Lia said, "or else we had better get used to murdering each other."

Gem snorted. "Should I not have already gotten used to that?"

Lia and Gem had been best friends since third grade—after an incident with the school-issued square pizza and May Barnard's face—and had been inseparable ever since, even though Gem's loathing for May had shifted to a crush this last year.

"Look at us!" Gem spun Lia to the mirror and rested their chin atop her head. "We're going to win."

A crack in the mirror split Lia's long face in half and made her green eyes uneven. Behind her, Gem's tall, muscled form was split and squished.

Their phones dinged with the same message:

Hello, Lia Prince & Gem Hastings.
Welcome to the game and happy hunting.
The Council

"Think this means we're on the same team?" Gem asked.

"Maybe." Lia shook her head, rubbed the back of her neck, and picked up her backpack. "It means that whoever the Council is knows us well enough to assume we're together right now."

"You know," Gem said, turning away, "even if we don't win, it'll be a good way to spend time together before next year."

"We'll win." Lia shook her head at her shattered image in the mirror. Gem won lots of things—best grades, theater tournaments, and test score competitions. The only award Lia had ever gotten was for attendance. "I just wish the Council told us everything up front."

No one knew who the Council was or how they were chosen, but the rumor was that it was three seniors handpicked by the previous year's Council. Everyone in Lincoln knew each other and their deepest secrets, so Lia had always assumed that rumor was true. The town was too small to keep such a mystery for so long.

"I bet it's Gabo," Gem said. "He loves stuff like this."

Gabriel Gutierrez, math genius and theater nerd, was one of Lia's guesses for the Council, too. His older brother had won Assassins seven years ago and had given him all his old notes. Gabriel even had a hand-me-down tricked-out water gun.

Mark, Lia's older brother, had placed third but had never told her anything helpful.

"Don't worry," Lia said. "The Council always teams up friends, families, and crushes to keep the real fighting to a minimum."

In the years before the Council became anonymous and focused more on the teammate and target assignments, friendships had been ruined and relationships dashed due to Assassins.

"I hope we get May as a target," Gem said as they joined the crush of students in the hall.

Seniors opened bathroom doors and tugged their friends inside. Lia kept an eye on the ones who vanished inside for only a minute, noting their names or descriptions. There were 317 seniors, and Lia had spent all last year figuring out who would play. She had been left with fifty definites.

She had documented their daily schedules and which classrooms they were in this semester. Her journal was filled to the edges with names, maps, and by-the-minute timetables. Lia clutched it to her chest and wound her way upstairs to the biology lab with Gem.

Gem opened the door. "Stalking everyone?"

Lia waved her journal. "Not everyone, and it's all stuff they say aloud. It's not like I'm following them home. Stalking makes it sound weird and illegal."

Once the game was on and Lia had her first target, she would be following them home, but even she knew that sounded creepy.

A student snorted behind Lia, and she turned. Faith Franklin was frowning at her, her eyes going from Lia's muddy shoes to the soda-stained journal in her hands.

"Not illegal, Prince," Faith said. She was always immaculate from her pin-straight brown hair to her pure white tennis shoes. "Definitely weird, though."

Lia hadn't bothered documenting Faith; the girl hated games as much as she hated mess. Faith sat at the first bench in the biology lab and pulled out a bullet journal bursting with stickers and notes. Hannah, who sat behind her, pulled out some new calligraphy pen to show her. Lia dropped her journal and half-chewed pen onto a bench next to Gem.

"She's so organized," Lia said. "I bet her closet is gorgeous."

"Don't worry." Gem pulled out their work and grinned. "Once we win the game, nothing will be able to hold us back. We'll be unrivaled."

Lia laughed. "I don't think they give scholarships out for fake-murdering classmates."

In class, Lia had always been very, very rivaled.

With AP exams looming and their fates soon to arrive in admission portals, everyone took to the lab with as much liveliness as the day-old sheep eyeballs they were dissecting. At the next table, Devon Diaz, Lia's oblivious crush since seventh grade, was the only one really following the steps of the lab and not just cutting the eye into tiny pieces. His fingers curled around the handle of his scalpel as if it were his violin bow, steady and sure of every move. He blew his black hair, a touch too long and curling at the ends, out of his eyes and rolled his shoulders back. Devon was sharper than any note he ever played, always wearing button-down shirts and dark jeans. He was put together and knew exactly what he wanted—all A's, pre-med, and no distractions. Like dating.

Specifically, like dating Lia.

Near the end of class, Gem leaned over and whispered, "If Devon's our target, will you be able to kill him?"

"Of course I could kill him," Lia said, already calculating how hard she would have to pull the trigger to let loose the least amount of water. "But he's not playing."

"Did you ask him?" Gem asked. "You never talk to him."

"Yes."

This was a lie. Lia hadn't asked him. She'd just watched him for months. They moved in similar but distant circles, and he liked talking about music and how math touched everything. Lia could listen to him talk for hours, and sometimes did when she happened upon him talking to someone else and she could listen from the other side of a corner or bookshelf. He had no interest in what she could talk about—escape rooms, games, and sometimes art—but he was always kind enough to listen to her anyway. He would nod and smile, nudging her to keep talking. He was too nice.

And he always laughed at her jokes no matter how goofy they were.

"I never thought you'd have the nerve," Gem whispered.

Lia held up the small Nerf pistol—accuracy over deluge—she had started carrying in her bag Monday to get used to the weight. She didn't want any surprises come Friday. She sprayed Gem once, only lightly on the shoe, and a few drops of water splattered across the floor. Abby looked up from the book in her lap across the aisle.

Lia shrugged and mouthed, "Sorry."

Abby covered her laughter with the book as Ms. Christie gathered their worksheets and took them across the hall to the classroom.

"I could hear you talking about me, you know," Devon said, turning around. He spun his scalpel across his knuckles like a pen. "If I was playing, I would take you out first."

CHAPTER 2

"That's not how the game works," Lia said through her embarrassment. Being so well prepared for Assassins gave her the courage she needed to talk to him. She knew him enough to know the smirk meant he was joking, but still. "If you were playing, I would put you out of your misery quickly."

"How kind of you," Devon said.

"Consider it your last chance to rub elbows with the trash people not in the top ten percent of the class," Lia said. "Your last chance to screw around before you find out about college."

Lia had no clue what she would do after graduation. Everything about Lia was average—mediocre grades, boring hobbies. Assassins was her last chance to prove she knew what she was doing.

"I already found out," he said. His mouth twitched, and he moved as if to run a hand through his hair before remembering he was wearing eyeball-soaked gloves and holding a scalpel. "I got a Governor's Scholarship. I'm taking the full ride to Hendrix."

Governor's Scholarships were coveted and a point of pride for parents. They more than covered tuition cost at the University of

Arkansas, and Hendrix covered the rest of tuition for any student who received the scholarship and enrolled with them. In reality, it was just a desperate attempt to keep kids in Arkansas. Or that was what Mark had said when he turned his down two years ago.

"Really?" Lia nearly shouted.

Devon laughed.

"What?" Faith sliced her eye straight through the sclera. "What did you get on the ACT? Who else got one?"

Lia wasn't the best student, but she was pretty sure they weren't supposed to bisect the whole eye.

"Thirty-six," mumbled Devon. He stripped off his gloves and glanced at Lia. "Who gets them is private, so you'd have to ask around."

"I definitely didn't," Lia said. She'd gotten a 27 and a talking-to about not taking things as seriously as her older brother. Mark had gotten a 32, but he had played basketball. Lia played no sports and had no excuses for scoring lower than him. "That's amazing!"

Devon grinned. "Thanks."

"Of course you scored perfectly," Faith muttered. Her face was blank, but she stripped off her gloves, doused her hands in hand sanitizer, and picked at her jagged nails until a little crescent peeled away. "The rest of us heathens will have to wait for our letters."

"I'm sure you're fine," Lia said.

Faith loved competition, especially the easy sort that showed she was better—wearing hundred-dollar sweatpants to public school, eating lunch with a full set of miniature metal silverware, and suggesting that the rest of them get tutors like her whenever they talked about testing nerves.

"With a thirty-two and a fifteen-ten, I had better be." Faith went back to her eyeball. "I did everything right. I'm not sure why I didn't get higher. What did you get, Prince? I was sure you'd miss it because you were stalking us for Assassins or something."

Lia rolled her lips together and couldn't even bring herself to answer.

"No one cares about those scores as much as you," Devon said. "Here—what do I need to do to sign up?"

He held out his phone to Lia. She pulled up the email she had sent to the Council and typed it word for word for him.

He leaned over her arm to read what she typed. "I don't have a water gun, and I'm not ready to be killed."

"You can borrow one of mine," she said. "Dear Council, I, Devon Diaz, would love to lose Assassins."

The bell for the end of first block rang. Devon hit SEND, and Lia got up, knocking over her open backpack, pens rolling away. He laughed and helped her pick them up.

"You should be more light-footed, master assassin," he said. "I'll text you to get that water gun."

"Finally getting that date, master assassin," Gem whispered.

Lia knocked her shoulder against theirs. "Shut up."

They wove their way through the halls to their next class, Lia noting every senior she knew leaving the bathroom with their phone in hand. As they sat down in their next class, Gem leaned against the window.

Outside, May Barnard and the other soccer girls sprinted across the lawn. They spent every Monday, Wednesday, and Friday first block at the gym down the street with the other varsity teams, and Lia was sure all of them would play Assassins. May was in the lead, her bright red hair streaming out behind her, and she threw her head back with laughter. She was pretty and perfect, and seemed to glow instead of sweat. Gem stared, mouth slightly open.

"This is serious. No romantic distractions." Lia rolled her eyes and took her seat. "And she's the reason you had in-school suspension for a week."

"Growth and change are important aspects of life, and she did apologize." Gem sighed and dropped their elbows to the sill, folding in on themselves like a dead spider's legs. "She does that thing where she rolls up her sleeves, so it's not like I could not like her. Look."

"She's not my type," Lia said, "but if she's our target, you don't have to help kill her."

"You're so kind," Gem said, and sighed. "I bet she could bench-press me."

Lia laughed. "Is that a thing?"

"I don't even care," Gem said. "And you're one to talk about romantic distractions."

Lia flushed. "No distractions at all. If we're not on a team, I love you, but you're dead to me."

Gem reached out and tapped the tip of Lia's nose. "I always wanted a nemesis."

The rest of class went as it usually did—boring—and halfway through, Lia added her new notes from her journal to the spreadsheet she kept just in case. It was always good to have a backup.

"There are definitely more people playing than I anticipated," Lia said.

Cassidy Clarke twisted around at her desk. "Did you stalk us?" she asked.

Lia froze.

"Oh my God," Gem said, pointing to the blue, pink, and

white hairclip keeping Cassidy's bun in place. "Where did you get this?"

"Online." Cassidy scrunched her mouth up and narrowed her eyes, returning her gaze to Lia. "Did you follow me around?"

"No," Lia said, and bit her cheek. "I did not follow you."

Lia had only taken notes on where Cassidy said she was going. That wasn't following.

"What about me?" Ryder asked, leaning around Cassidy to stare at Lia.

Lia pretended to check her journal and clucked her tongue. "I'm sorry. Who are you?"

"You liar." Cassidy laughed, turned back around, and shook her head. "You better not win."

CHAPTER 3

Two days later, a hush fell over the cafeteria as noon neared, the silence so odd even Mr. Jackson, Lincoln's sole security guard, looked up from his crossword. Of all the seniors Lia could see, at least half were bent over their phones.

At exactly noon, she got the message.

> Hello, Lia Prince.
> Welcome to Assassins. Your goal is to kill your targets with your team without being seen, and survive until only one is left alive. However, as with all good things, there are rules:
>
> 1. Kills must have (mostly) no witnesses. You are an assassin, an enigma wrapped in shadows and trailing mystery. You must be sneaky. All kills must be committed when the target is completely alone, and no one except your team members can see you kill your target. If you kill

someone who is not alone, the kill will not be legitimate. Also, they'll know you have it out for them.

2. Kills must be made with water guns, and the guns may only be filled with water. Any amount of water on clothes or skin is enough to kill the target, so don't go overboard. Don't modify paintballs and don't aim for the face—we don't want a repeat of three years ago.

3. Shields are allowed, but they must obviously be a shield. Your arm is not a shield; your backpack is.

4. Self-defense is allowed. If an assassin attempts to kill you and fails or you notice them first, you may kill them.

5. Do not commit a crime in order to kill your target. You will be arrested or worse, disqualified.

6. The school is a safe zone. No kills can be made on school grounds during school hours, and any that are made will get you disqualified.

7. Do not camp at your house to avoid death. Anyone who refuses to leave their house for more than three days in a row will be disqualified. Anyone who makes their parents follow them around for more than three days in a row will be disqualified. Do not pay non-players to follow you around. You will be disqualified. The game is about teamwork and survival as much as it is killing. You have your team for a reason.

8. When you kill your target, email 9781579126247@gmail.com that you have

completed your contract. The Council will provide
you with a new target by the next midnight.

9. If you are killed and would like to dispute it, email
9781579126247@gmail.com with your evidence
of a disqualifying kill. The council will decide
within a reasonable amount of time.

10. Once there are only three assassins remaining,
we will inform them of their accomplishment.

11. And the most important rule of all—have fun!

12. We're kidding. Murder is a necessity. Fun is
optional.

Your team members are Ben Barnard, Gem Hastings,
and Devon Diaz. If you don't already have them,
phone numbers and addresses are in the student
directory.
Your first target is Abby Ascher.
The game begins in five hours. Remember: you're
someone's target too.
Good luck,
The Council
PS: OBVIOUSLY NONE OF THIS IS LITERAL.
DON'T KILL ANYONE. NO DANGEROUS TRAPS.
PUTTING ANOTHER ASSASSIN IN DANGER WILL
DISQUALIFY YOU. IF YOU HURT ANYONE OR
DAMAGE ANY PROPERTY, YOU'RE ON YOUR OWN.

"Well," Lia said, laying her face on the plastic lattice table
smothered in decades of student germs. "Devon's going to be sad
he can't kill me."

"No. Romantic. Distractions." Gem pulled her up. "Gabo definitely didn't write that last part. He hates caps."

So the Council was still a mystery, then, but at least one concerned about legality.

Lia threaded her fingers through the table lattice. "Ben's good, though, and he always goes all in."

"I can't believe your terrible flirting convinced Devon to play," Gem said. "He's walking over here, by the way."

Devon usually ate with a handful of orchestra kids. He walked through the crowd toward their table. "Why do I feel like you set this up?" he said, dropping his bag onto the bench next to Lia and crossing his arms.

"Are any of the other orchestra kids playing?" Lia asked. "They group friends and classmates together."

"Yeah," Gem said, "we can't have you and the second violin bitter about Assassins for the rest of the year after she kills you."

He shook his head. "Most of them aren't. We have rehearsal every night for the spring concert. It's too easy to take us out."

"Well, now you have us and Ben to protect you." Lia smiled. "Did you read the rules?"

"Yes, but I'm assuming you have it all planned out. You love things like this," Devon said.

Lia *did* love things like this—tabletop games, escape rooms . . . anything that relied on strategy and not luck—but how did he know that?

"Do I talk about it too much?" Lia asked. She talked about it sometimes. Maybe that was how he knew.

"No, you smile when you talk about things you like." Devon

read over the email again, his nose crinkling. "What happened three years ago?"

"Someone modded a paintball gun to shoot water balls that would pop on impact." Lia held up her bio notebook and pointed to her labeled sketch of an eye. "Mark said the shooter hit a kid in the eye and got disqualified."

She said it in a whisper. No one ever got disqualified. To be kicked out of the game was to be the ultimate buzzkill and loser. Getting disqualified meant you had done something bad enough to get removed *and* put the game in danger of being shut down. Disqualified kids were basically outcasts for the rest of the school year. Lia would die before suffering disqualification.

The kid who had been hit had deferred his first year of college. Lia's older brother, Mark, had gotten third place that year, betraying his best friend on the final day. It wasn't an academic achievement, but their parents had still been proud. Their pride only grew when college decisions came in.

He'd gotten scholarships and a special dinner. He'd gotten into MIT and been gifted a new car. Lia had gotten eighteen years of parents and teachers comparing her to him. She was always "Mark's sister."

Not this year. This year, she'd be better. If they had been proud of him for Assassins, they could be proud of her, even if it was only a game.

"Your priorities amaze me," Devon said.

"Why?" she asked, raising an eyebrow.

"The kid could have died, and you're concerned about them still being counted 'out' in the game." He looked at her and smiled. "You'd murder me in a heartbeat, wouldn't you?"

"Only metaphorically." Lia leaned back against the table. She had teased a smile out of Devon Diaz! Twice in three days! Sure, they had all been about murder, but that counted. "I would've made it a fun murder."

"At least neither of you have to worry about it now," Gem said. "Ben usually trains during lunch, so we'll have to talk to him later."

Impulsively, Lia uncapped her pen with her mouth and drew her phone number on Devon's hand.

"Text me after school," she said. "I'll send out the plan."

"Great." He ran his thumb across the ink. "Can't wait to win."

Lia's skin prickled at the easy way he trusted her.

The moment he was out of earshot, Lia grabbed Gem's arm. "Was he being sarcastic?"

"I don't think so," Gem said. "I've never seen you romantically distracted. This'll be fun."

"This will be perfect." Lia pulled up her schedule of all the seniors' movements—when they got to school, their classes, where they ate lunch, when they left and how, and what they did after—and scrolled to Ben's section. "He has a thirty-minute break between school and practice, and practice ends at four-thirty on Fridays. I'll send out the plan then. Think we can get him tomorrow?"

"I've got nothing tonight and tomorrow, and then family brunch Sunday," Gem said. "Rusty is ours."

Rusty was the old red Saturn Gem shared with their younger sister, and it ran fine but looked rough after fifteen years. Gem was the only one with access to a car, though.

"Good. That'll be safer," Lia said.

Lia created a group text for her, Gem, Devon, and Ben.

Tomorrow we follow Abby. Gem and I will pick up
Ben at 5:45 AM and Devon at 6:00 AM. Be ready. I'll
explain the plan then.

She was taking charge of the team, but someone had to, and if
anyone was qualified, it was her.

Ben sent back sixty-nine exclamation points.

A few minutes later Devon texted back.

You still owe me a water gun, Prince

Blue, green, or yellow?

Surprise me

CHAPTER 4

The next morning, Gem and Lia met in Gem's driveway at five, and Lia waved to the yawning Mrs. Hastings, who was standing at the door. Lia wore black leggings, an old blue sweatshirt, and running shoes. Her hair was in a ponytail, and the only makeup she wore was mascara and some lip balm. It was easy for Lia to go unnoticed; she was middling. She doubted the assassin who had her name even knew what she looked like. Not that she was leaving her survival to chance; her neighbor walked her dog every morning at five, rain or shine, and Lia had walked over with her.

"I can't believe you have the whole senior class tracked," Gem said. "It's creepy."

"Which is why I'm not telling anyone," Lia said as they got in the car. She scrolled through her spreadsheets. "And all the information I have, people blabbed about freely. It's not like I hacked their calendars."

Lincoln was a strip of hilly, boggy, foresty land in the way that only Arkansas could be, and the car wound its way from the dark streets that were too remote to warrant streetlights to the well-lit stretch of perfectly manicured lawns along Highway 10. Gem and Lia lived in the center of Lincoln, and their neighborhood was a mix of lower-middle-class people and people pretending to be middle class and ignoring the rising costs of their area. Ben's family was new money, and he lived a good twenty minutes from Gem. White stone columns and peaked roofs replaced the skyline of evergreens and listing power lines.

Gem pulled up to a large house whose yard was littered with sports equipment, and several minutes later Ben jogged out the front door as if he woke up before dawn for elaborate water-gun assassinations every morning.

"'Sup," he said, and tucked all six feet three inches of himself and his modded-for-distance water gun into the backseat behind Lia. He wore all black and had covered his Lincoln-Lions-red hair with a black beanie. "May said most of the soccer team isn't playing, but track is. Hope y'all are in shape."

"Is May playing?" Gem asked.

"I'm not my sister's keeper." Ben grinned and snapped the bands of his braces with his tongue. "Guess you'll have to be brave and ask her yourself. May doesn't like cowards."

"Be nice," Lia said, knowing how Gem felt. "Is May in the game or not?"

Gem's light brown skin reddened around their cheeks and ears. By the time they had pulled into Devon's small neighborhood tucked behind an old cemetery and the new Starbucks, Gem's face was practically heating the car.

"Yeah, fine," Gem said. "I get that she doesn't like cowards. But . . . would she like *me*?"

"What?" Ben asked.

Gem glared at him in the rearview mirror.

"Oh." Ben nodded, understanding. "Hell yeah."

"Great." Lia patted Gem's arm. "Just don't be a coward."

"I'm going to murder you," Gem whispered, and unlocked the doors.

Devon, a scarf pulled up around his chin, crawled into the seat behind Gem. "My face isn't used to being up before dawn," he said, yawning.

"Here's the deal." Lia turned to them, using her arm to hide the bleach spots on her sweatshirt. She had dressed for Assassins, but Devon looked impeccable. The ass. "I know every senior's schedule, so we're good if they don't change that. Our new rules to live by are one, go nowhere alone, and two, practice your aim." She looked at Ben. "Will you be okay at gym before school if we don't pick you up?"

He nodded. "Never alone. And if I am . . ." He pulled open his coat and revealed two water guns Velcroed to the lining.

"Devon?" Lia asked.

"I'm assuming you and Gem will be picking me up?" he asked, one black brow arched. "My mother will be delighted about not sharing the car."

"Great," Lia said. "We should get Abby quickly. Once a few targets are killed this first weekend, people will get more paranoid. It'll be better if we can kill Abby and then get to our next target quickly before people start changing their schedules. We'll also learn who the competition really is," Lia said. She held out a neon-green water gun to him. "Sound good?"

"Still slightly creepy." Devon held up the water gun and checked the seal against the water sloshing inside. "I love green. This isn't filled with caffeine, is it?"

"Only water," Lia said. "Sorry."

"It's fine." He held up his thumb and forefinger. "It only lessens my love a little."

Lia ignored the flutter in her stomach. "As you know, our target is Abby Ascher. What you don't know is that she goes for a walk with her dog Omelet to Pleasant Pines and then she runs home before heading to work a few hours later."

Lia hadn't needed to follow Abby to know that. They lived near enough that her dad always joked about setting his watch by Abby's morning run, even though all the watches he owned were digital.

"Oh my God," whispered Ben, "she named her dog Omelet."

"I know. It's good." Lia handed them each a printout of what she knew of Abby's schedule. "Ideally, we'll get her today, but if we don't, there's tomorrow morning or when she gets off work tomorrow."

"Did you follow everyone?" Ben asked, his face scrunching up.

"Not everyone," Lia said quickly.

Devon scanned the paper and whistled. "Your preparedness is terrifying."

"It's color-coded, but the printer sucks." Lia gestured to his dark jeans and sweater. "Are you okay with those getting wet?"

"They won't," he said. "I refuse to die."

"You need anything to blend in more?" Ben asked. He emptied one of his pockets, pulling free three granola bars, a collapsible water bottle, a ski mask, a sewing kit, an EpiPen, a flashlight, and three gum wrappers. "I came prepared."

"Sure did," muttered Gem, maneuvering the car into an empty spot a few blocks away from Abby's house.

"Brown boy in a ski mask in the dark?" Devon said with both eyebrows raised. "Yeah, no thanks."

Gem saluted Devon in the rearview mirror. "Who's the EpiPen for? You allergic to anything?"

"Oh yeah, but it's embarrassing," Ben said, and laughed. "I'm allergic to latex. Makes me look like a lobster and as good at breathing air. May and I both carry one just in case."

Lia added that to the top of her journal page on Ben in all caps. "Why is that embarrassing?"

"You know." He flushed as red as his hair. "Guy stuff."

Devon, holding back laughter, patted Ben's arm.

Lia checked her phone. "Abby should be leaving her house soon. If I were alone, I would get her at her house, but I figured this would be more fun. We can take positions around the path."

They slunk out of the car. Lia looked around her, a pair of binoculars pressed to her eyes. Shadows danced in the dark between the trees, limbs grasping at the air, and a woodpecker picked at a waterlogged fence post. The posts had marked the boundaries of the old park, but as the waterline of the creek winding through the area had grown, they had been lost. Now an old bridge arched over them, connecting the walking paths to the newer dog park.

The four kids took up spots a little ways off the path. As Abby walked Omelet around the park, they would shoot her when she neared. Lia knelt in the cold next to Gem. Devon sat beside her.

"Did you stalk me?" he asked.

"It wasn't stalking, and no. I didn't think you would play," Lia said. "It's not like I watched people through windows."

Devon laughed, and Gem held a finger up to their lips. Leaves rustled in the late winter breeze. Lia rubbed the back of her neck.

From the dimly lit street came Abby and Omelet. Gem gestured to Lia, miming a shot. Lia pulled a slightly larger water gun from her backpack. She was hoping the longer barrel would help her aim. She had spent most of winter break practicing. Abby paused on the bridge, and Lia took aim. Abby stretched her arms over her head.

Lia fired. The water arched for Abby, perfectly on target. Omelet, a big Alaskan malamute, rose to his hind legs and lunged for Abby's face, tongue lolling. Water splattered against his side. Startled, he pushed hard on her shoulders. Abby leapt back.

"Good start," Devon whispered.

Lia groaned. "Crap."

A sickening crack silenced them all. Abby teetered on the edge of the bridge, her arms thrown back, and plummeted through the railing. She vanished beneath the bridge.

CHAPTER 5

Omelet yowled. The gun slipped from Lia's hand. Gem inhaled sharply, their hand brushing Lia's arm. Lia sprinted for Abby, the others crashing behind her, and wove between the old posts leading to the bridge. She ducked under the bridge and nearly tripped over Abby's sprawled legs.

"Abby!" Lia crouched down next to her. She lay faceup in the mud. "Are you okay?"

Abby turned her head to stare at Lia and then glanced down at the old fence post right next to her side. "I think so?"

"Abby!" Devon stumbled to a stop, Gem and Ben at his heels. "Is she okay?"

"Can you sit up? Wait, can you move your legs? Did you hit your head?" Lia gently touched her shoulder. The post had torn through her coat and shirt, leaving a trail of splinters from Abby's elbow to her wrist. Lia winced. "Your arm—"

"Yeah," Abby said, gaze stuck on it. "That could have been really bad."

"But for real." Devon knelt on Abby's other side and checked the rest of her for cuts. "Does anything else hurt?"

"My pride?" Abby frowned and wiggled her feet. "I think I'm fine. Did you shoot Omelet?"

"Yeah, sorry about that," Lia said. "And this."

Abby shifted, and Lia helped her sit up. Ben dug through his pockets and handed Devon three bandages, some tweezers, and hand sanitizer.

"Thanks," Devon said, "but doing this ourselves is probably a bad idea."

Lia swallowed. "How mad are your parents going to be?"

"It's not that bad, so a little mad maybe." Abby turned her arm over, and above them on the bridge Omelet whined. "I'm okay, buddy. Sit."

Omelet sat, and Ben scrambled up the slight embankment to grab him.

"Well," Abby said, "this is an exciting start to Assassins."

"Do you think they'll cancel it?" Lia asked.

Devon eyed her with a look that said *Seriously?* "Priorities, Lia. Priorities."

"Sorry." She sighed. "I'm just saying that would suck."

And it would all have been for nothing. She would have nothing left. Nothing after what happened last year.

"Sorry," Lia repeated. She stood and picked up the bridge railing that had given way. The push had yanked a handful of nails free, but it hadn't broken when it fell. The nails glittered in the grass around Abby. Lia moved one away from where she was sitting. The wood looked worn down around the holes. The nails must have been loose. "But it's not like the game is why she fell."

"It sort of is, though," Devon said. He helped Abby move her torn sleeves out of the way. "It's not that deep."

"I don't think it's that bad," Abby said slowly. "I definitely need it cleaned, but I don't want to be the girl who got Assassins cancelled."

Lia sighed. "I am really, really sorry you fell."

It wasn't that Lia *wasn't* sorry—she was—but the idea of the game being canceled over something even moderately her fault broke her skin out in goose bumps.

She sat next to Abby. A few broken fingernails were around her feet. Okay. Lia was sorry about that. That had to hurt.

"Gem, can you pull your car up as close to the park entrance as possible?" Lia asked.

"Yeah, yeah." Gem took off.

"Do you think if you move, it'll get worse?" Devon asked.

Abby shook her head. "Don't let Omelet jump down here."

"You good, then?" Ben asked, peeking over the bridge. "I can walk him to your house and meet you there?"

Lia texted Ben the address to Abby's house. She helped Devon pull Abby to her feet, taking care of the injured arm. Abby hooked her good arm over Devon, and Lia helped support the other. Her hands shook softly, but Abby didn't seem to notice. Abby wrinkled her nose at the bridge as they passed it.

"I always grab that railing to stretch," Abby said. "I tie the leash to it, too. Good thing I didn't today."

"The nails looked loose." Lia squeezed her hand. "I am sorry."

Abby laughed. "I know. Let's just not make this a habit."

They got her to Gem's car and tucked her into the front seat, maneuvering the seat belt for her. Devon and Lia crawled into the backseat.

"So," Abby said, looking at each of them. "I don't want to get the school involved—everyone would hate me—but you owe me."

Lia leaned back in her seat. "Yeah?"

"Technically, what just happened was property damage," Abby continued. "You could get disqualified if the Council found out."

Lia opened her mouth but couldn't form the words. Gem winced.

"Yeah," Abby said, dragging it out. "If I told, you could get disqualified, and that would really be terrible."

Fear clamped Lia's mouth shut, so Devon was the one who had to break the silence.

"Are you trying to extort us?" he asked. "You already had the upper hand."

"I almost had no hand." Abby hummed. "Oh my God, Prince, lighten up. You take this game way too seriously. I won't tell anyone about this if you all agree to not kill me for a week."

They would be so far behind the other teams if they waited to go after Abby until next weekend, but she had a point. The game would still be on. If they were disqualified, they were done for in the game and in real life.

"That seems fair?" Devon said, pitching the statement like a question.

Gem nodded. "I would like to not be disqualified."

"And being the people who got adults involved with the game seems less than fun," Devon said.

Lia *had* shot Abby's dog and sent her tumbling off a bridge, and bore part of the responsibility for hurting her. It was fair. A week was more than enough time to figure out their new plan of attack.

"It is fair," Lia said grudgingly.

The car pulled in front of Abby's house. Outside, the malamute rolled over, dirt caking his wet fur. Ben laughed and took a picture.

Abby sighed. "Maybe also help me wash him?" she asked.

Devon glanced at Lia. She nodded.

"Yeah," Lia said. "I'll do that while you get your arm checked out. Do we have a deal?"

"I don't tell anyone this was related to the game, you don't get disqualified, I get to breathe freely for a week, and I don't have to wash Omelet?" Abby grinned and stuck out her good hand. "Deal."

Lia took her hand, a plan already forming in her mind.

CHAPTER 6

Abby's parents weren't terribly mad. Her mom was mostly worried about infection, her dad about scarring. They let Lia into the backyard to wash the mud off Omelet, and Gem drove Ben home. Devon stuck around to help with Omelet.

"So I guess today was a wash," Lia said, holding Omelet in place as Devon unknotted a twig from his fur.

Devon laughed. "We can get a clean start next week."

Lia stroked the damp fur on Omelet's other side. Omelet let out a soft *ah-woo*. "She'll be okay, right?" Lia asked.

"Are you asking because you're worried about her or because you're worried about someone connecting it to Assassins?" he asked, and tossed the twig away. "I know I said it jokingly, but your priorities are a little weird."

He picked out the last of Omelet's muddy mats—Lia was sure Omelet hadn't been this muddy when he left the park with Ben, but she could blame Ben for letting him roll about—and the dog whined.

"I know, but you're such a good boy," Devon mumbled. A

31

squirrel leapt along the fence around Abby's backyard, and Omelet tensed. "Don't even think about it, egg."

"Egg?" Lia asked.

"He's a good egg," Devon said. "I can't believe you shot him and then let Abby make a deal with you."

"It was her idea." Lia frowned. She wasn't sure how to read Devon—he had joked with her, but he also seemed a little mad about the whole thing. Sometimes she wished people came with handbooks.

Devon Diaz: loves puns, baby talks to dogs, and will judge you for loving Assassins too much.

"Of course I was more worried about Abby." And that was true—Lia's hands had been trembling by the time they had gotten to Abby's house. "But once I knew she was fine, I started thinking ahead. This game is determined in seconds and minutes, not days. We needed to know right then what would happen or else all our plans would've been useless."

Abby was easygoing, but she could have died. Lia had needed to take advantage of any good feelings Abby had before she found out for sure if she needed stitches.

"Sure, but it's still just a game," Devon said. "I've never seen you this into something."

Devon was into acceptable things—music and medicine. Lia's interests—video and table-top games—were things her parents definitely didn't understand. They could brag about her brother's soccer and his stellar grades, but with Lia, there was nothing to brag about.

"It's just . . ." Lia shrugged, sucked on her teeth, and shook her head. She started rubbing Omelet dry. "You wouldn't get it. You're good at things."

"I'm good at things because I work at them," he said.

"I work so hard at so many things," Lia said, her voice rising. She took a breath. "When you say that, it sounds like you're implying that I don't work at things. Like I don't practice. Like I'm lazy."

Lia tried and tried, but by the time the secrets to Calculus AB or chemistry made sense to her, the class was already on to some other new subject and Lia's grade was a solid 75 percent. But with Assassins, she knew her classmates and the town, and she knew how games like this worked. She had finally had all the time she needed to prep. She could finally be good at something.

"Sorry. I really didn't mean it like that." He finished drying Omelet off. "People say stuff to me all the time. They tell me I'm so lucky I'm good at music or that I have an ear for it." He made a face. "I spent years practicing. They only ever see the outcome, never all the failures." Then he looked at Lia. "You're not failing at anything," he said. "I've been in half your classes."

"Yeah, but I'm not good at them either. Ms. Christie had to ask my name three weeks ago, and I've had her for two classes." Lia patted Omelet's head and shrugged. "I'm really good at games, and they're never important. This one is. It's the only thing that Lincoln cares about that I'm good at."

And her parents were part of Lincoln. The adults of the town might turn a blind eye to the antics of Assassins, but they respected the tradition. She had always known her parents were disappointed in her, but this was a chance to make them proud.

"I see where you get your mixed-up priorities now." Devon pulled away from Omelet and gently draped the towel over his head like a veil. Omelet woofed and flicked his head back. "So the game is *really* important to you, huh?"

Lia nodded.

"I guess I should try harder, then," he said.

A pleasant warmth fluttered in her chest and she smiled. "Thank you. And I promise not to shoot anyone else off a bridge."

• ●

It was an easy promise to keep. By Monday, Abby's injury was common knowledge. How she got it was not.

"She was teaching Omelet to box," Georgia said. She sat next to Abby in every class they had together. "Omelet won."

Abby rolled her eyes and stole a piece of Georgia's breakfast bar. "Lia and Gem were there. They saw Omelet best me."

"He has a mean uppercut," Gem said. "How's your arm?"

"It still hurts," Abby said. "The cops showed up."

"They did?" Lia asked nervously.

Abby nodded. "They said someone had vandalized the bridge. And by someone they meant me."

"Why would anyone vandalize that bridge?" Lia asked. There were too many nosy neighbors for vandalism to turn out well. "Why would you?"

"I think they thought I was trying to set a trap for Assassins." Abby leaned back and prodded the brace on her wrist. "My mom told them that bridge had messed me up, so the city could expect a letter about medical bills."

"You're too kindhearted for traps," Lia said, and swung her backpack around. The mesh was terrible for keeping secrets, and Abby laughed before Lia had even finished pulling the water gun free. "Since you're still alive, I thought you could use this."

Lia had modded the barrel to be more accurate—hopefully— over long distances, and the tank held just enough for five shots so that it wasn't too heavy to lift quickly. Her dad had complained about the melted plastic smell that hung around the backyard as Lia worked on it, but the outcome was worth it.

Abby took it with the reverence she usually reserved for dogs and books. "Did you make this?" she asked, and when Lia nodded, she grinned. "It's such cheap plastic. How did you not just break it?"

"Oh, no, I broke a few before this one worked out." Lia tapped the neon-blue tip. "It's way more accurate than normal, and light enough for you to use with only one arm."

Abby laughed and tucked it into her bag as her teacher walked in. "I wasn't expecting this. Thank you."

"Of course," Lia said. She needed to keep Abby happy for now.

Lia had heard three different accounts of how Abby had hurt her arm before lunch, and all of them featured the game. More than a few students whispered furiously about how breaking the bridge could mess it up for all of them. Lia sank down into her seat at the lunch table.

"How can you be so good at poker and have such a bad poker face?" Gem pulled out their lunch. "What's your plan?"

"Let's wait for Devon," Lia said, pointing toward his lithe frame dodging the elbows and yellow lunch trays of the crowd outside the cafeteria.

"I heard about Abby's fight with a vandalizing freshman," he said instead of greeting them.

Lia yanked open a bag of Flamin' Hot Cheetos. "I thought she assassinated the Council."

"Obviously not," Gem said, "because we all know the truth—Omelet's a werewolf."

"Okay, I hadn't heard that one." Devon sat down next to Lia, his leg a mere few inches from hers, and pulled out a squat thermos filled with soup. Steam fogged up his glasses when he unscrewed the top. "Regardless, people are a bit nervous about the Council canceling the game."

"They wouldn't cancel," Lia said quickly.

"They would if the cops got involved," Gem said. "One year canceled is better than all future years banned."

"Abby seems happy to play along so far," Lia said. Her Cheeto-dusted fingers left orange prints on the table as she fidgeted. "I can't believe her arm was fractured. The fall tore out some of her nails, you know."

"I definitely checked out her hand, and she had all her nails unless she's been hiding extras." Devon leaned back. "It was just an accident. If anything, whoever is in charge of the park is responsible."

"Most of the adults in town played Assassins. They know the deal," Lia said. "We need to decide what to do once our week is up and we can go after her."

"She'll change her schedule," Devon said. "The one you know."

Lia stared at him. "Obviously."

Assassins was hers. It hurt that Devon didn't know she knew that, as if she weren't able to figure it out. Abby would return to her walks soon, fractured arm or no. She was as picky about her walks with Omelet as she was about her books; she had cried in fourth grade when Sam Allen dog-eared a page in her favorite novel.

"There's a reason I agreed to her deal, you know," Lia said. "Even if you can't figure it out."

Devon downed the last of his soup, and behind the lip of his thermos, his mouth curled up.

"You liked watching me fail, didn't you?" Lia asked, frowning.

"Aside from the fact that Abby fell, it was a little funny," Devon said, smirking. "Admit it."

Lia groaned. "I only missed because Omelet tackled her."

"And you didn't observe the whims of dogs and write them down with a full appendix?" He clutched his heart. "I'm disappointed. I could set up a target in my backyard, and you could come practice if you think it would help."

He grinned as he said it, and a flickering heat filled her chest till her words felt hot and heavy.

"Are you inviting me over?" she asked.

"Actually, I was planning on betraying you and using you for target practice as revenge for getting me caught up in this." He looked away. "Of course."

"Of course," Lia said, smiling. "I suppose I'll just have to prove my worth this week."

CHAPTER 7

On Monday night, Lia made plans instead of sleeping. Her parents had been strict with Mark, but Lia was the second child. They had exhausted all their helicoptering, he used to say, and she was lucky they didn't watch her like a hawk. They spent more time worrying about her on the Parents of Lions Facebook group than talking to her about her life. Really, Lia knew he just mattered more, so they paid less attention to her.

She left the house at five a.m. on Tuesday. Her parents snored right through it. She wasn't going to kill Abby. They had made a deal, after all. She was just going to follow Abby and see if she kept her normal routine. She had nothing to fear, but maybe she would scope out new routes or invite a friend to journey out with her and Omelet. It was the perfect time for Abby to experiment with ways to stay alive in Assassins, which meant it was the perfect time for Lia to figure out how to get around those ways. The water gun she had gifted Abby would make it harder, especially now that Abby was on alert, but it would be a good challenge.

If she killed Abby, people would know how good she was.

Devon, too, might not feel the need to remind her of obvious things.

Abby lived a good twenty-minute walk from Lia's, and in the quiet dark before dawn, no one was about. Frosted grass blades snapped underfoot, leaving an inky trail behind her as she cut across yards and little neighborhood parks. No one locked their gates in Lincoln. Lia's parents had only started locking theirs after binging five true-crime podcasts last summer.

Abby's house was a peak-roofed shadow backlit by a neighbor's motion lights. Lia waited across the street, huddled against a brick mailbox. Lia didn't know Abby's full schedule, but she knew Abby would walk Omelet no matter what. So she waited.

The motion lights switched off. The wind sliced through Lia's scarf, burning in her nose. A fence creaked, wood rubbing against wood, and a car passed on the adjacent street. Light flitted through the hedges and houses, washing the windows of Abby's house white, and the motion lights switched on again. Omelet's soft *ah-woo* echoed across the quiet street. A light flickered on behind a covered window of the Ascher house, and a door slammed shut. Abby and Omelet emerged from the dark backyard.

Omelet's safety vest glowed, and Abby reached up to turn on a lamp attached to her ear warmers. The brace on her arm was a bulge beneath her white sweatshirt.

They started off power walking. Abby kept one eye on the windows of her house until she turned the corner. Another early morning runner sprinted down a parallel street, setting off lights and yappy dogs, and Lia sighed. Lia crept after them, keeping close to the shadows between the streetlights.

"Maybe we'll run a little," Abby said, and scratched the malamute's head. "Don't tell Dr. Kim."

And they were off, two ghosts racing down the streets toward the park. Lia couldn't keep up. She wasn't sporty, and even if she was, her footsteps would have been too loud. She didn't need to follow Abby closely anyway. She only needed to know which paths Abby took.

She followed the *slap-slap* of Abby's tennis shoes against the pavement to the rougher concrete of the park. Spindly trees crackled in the breeze, and Lia ducked into the safety of their trunks to hide, using her phone to see. She added "long path" to her notes about Abby. It was the one that didn't cross the bridge.

Slap-slap, ah-whoo.

The path wound through the narrow section of woods at the edge of the neighborhood, making the park seem bigger and more forested than it really was. It felt like some backwoods haven miles away from Lincoln.

Slap-slap, ah-whoo.

Lia crunched through the grass at the edge of the cracked concrete. Abby and Omelet began to round the bend, and Lia no longer had to creep so much. Someone was probably following Lia and pissed they couldn't shoot her since she was too near Abby. During Assassins, few people went out alone, but Lia didn't mind being alone. She had grown used to the loneliness. Mark was the sort of brother who was more apt to measure the Snickers they were about to split with a ruler than actually do things with Lia, and next year, Gem would be gone. Abby was just another classmate who knew what they wanted and had the means to get it. Lia hated the envy burning in her veins.

Slap-slap, woof.

Lia could barely even hear Abby and Omelet now. She started

jogging, one ear tilted out of the wind to listen. Lia should have walked faster—everyone outpaced her eventually.

Omelet barked. Then came a *thunk,* as if Abby had kicked a rock. A groan, tree limbs bent back too far by the wind. Damp branches splitting underfoot.

Then Abby took off again.

Lia ran after her. Maybe Abby had seen her lurking in the trees. Lia neared a sharp bend in the path, Omelet's bark growing louder and louder. Lia lengthened her strides, water gun in hand. She sprinted beneath a burned-out streetlight.

And tripped.

She went down hard. Her hands shot out and the water gun skidded across the sidewalk. Her chin smacked into her outstretched arm, teeth biting through her cheek. Gravel tore through the knees of her jeans. Lia groaned and rolled onto her side, eyes squeezing shut. Omelet whoofed and panted. He padded back and forth across the pavement. Lia shook her head.

"Not funny, Abby," Lia murmured, crawling to get the gun. Everything ached, and her right ankle throbbed. There was a ringing in her ears. "Abby?"

No one answered. Omelet, still pacing across the path in front of her, whined. The path was empty in both directions.

This had to be payback for the bridge, but Lia had never thought Abby was the revenge type.

"Abby?" The skin on Lia's hands looked like it had gotten the meanest rug burn she'd ever seen. "I don't think I fractured anything, but we're definitely even and you're freaking Omelet out."

Lia froze. The silence pressed in.

Abby would never leave Omelet like this, even if she were out for vengeance. Lia stumbled to her feet, and Omelet darted to the side of the path. Without the streetlight, Lia could only see his white fur. A dark stain marred his snout and paws.

Lia lurched after him. Abby lay off the path, facedown in the dirt. Her neck was twisted at an awkward angle.

"Abby!" Lia dropped to her knees and turned her over.

Blood soaked Abby's face, all of her red and warm and still. It thawed the frost on the ground in a halo around her. It darkened the indent where her skull had been cracked open and stuck to Lia's hands. It dripped down the rock that had broken Abby's fall. Lia's fingers fluttered near her jaw, desperate to find a pulse.

Nothing.

CHAPTER 8

In the dark, alone with Abby while the 911 operator barked instructions, Lia saw eyes peering out from the darkness. She saw shadows darting toward her down the path. She saw the bloodstain on Omelet's fur grow and cover him. She saw everything, none of it real.

The flashing lights from the arriving ambulance didn't help.

An EMT bundled Lia up in a silvery blanket and sat her on the path far from Abby. The path wasn't wide enough for cars, so they had all come running through the woods, cutting straight across the park. The sun was only just rising, and all of them were washed in red. Abby's parents arrived as the EMT finished cleaning her knee. A detective loomed behind them.

They talked to her and she answered, but she had no idea what she said. She had no idea what they said.

No, she hadn't seen it happen.

No, she hadn't been running with Abby.

Yes, they were playing that game and she was stalking Abby.

"I was just following a little ways behind, and then I heard . . . I thought . . ." Lia sniffed. "I thought she had kicked a rock or stubbed her toe, because I couldn't hear her running, and then Omelet was howling, and I tripped on something, and then Omelet came over to me, and I knew Abby wouldn't leave Omelet. She'd never leave Omelet, so I stood up and—"

"You tripped too?" one of the cops asked.

Too? Abby ran everywhere. She couldn't die from tripping.

Lia nodded, and a detective in a neat suit and wool coat glanced at her over the rim of his glasses.

Lia nodded. "It took me a minute to get up, and Omelet came over."

Lia's dad talked to the cops while her mom herded her to the car.

"Abby ran all the time," Lia said softly, an ache that had nothing to do with her wounds spreading through her.

"She wasn't supposed to be running," Lia's mom said. Her arm was tight around Lia's shoulders, and her lips were set in a hard, thin line. "You shouldn't have been out either."

"Sorry."

Her mom sighed and hugged Lia to her side. "No, no, it's fine. I'm just glad you're okay."

They passed a crowd of onlookers, old neighbors bundled up in dressing gowns beneath puffy coats and people on the way to work clutching travel mugs in their hands. Nothing worth gossiping about ever happened in Lincoln, but an ambulance and a cop car at dawn must've been worth talking about. Lia tucked her face into her mom's shoulder.

"So senseless." Lia's mom stroked her hair and tucked her into the back of their car. "Her poor parents. I was just talking to her mom yesterday. And for Abby to just . . ."

Lia could still remember the soft thrill in Abby's voice as she told Omelet that maybe they would run a little.

"It's not Abby's fault," Lia said quickly. "Even if she wasn't supposed to be running, it's not her fault."

Her mom reached back from the front seat and took her hand. "Of course it isn't. It's just so senseless. She had so much ahead of her—she just got that full ride, you know. And now—"

"I don't want to do this," Lia said. "I don't want to talk about this."

Her stomach dropped. How could she have been so jealous of Abby? She was terrible.

Her dad opened the door and climbed into the driver's seat before her mom could respond. "Home first, and if your head starts hurting, the hospital. Got it?"

Lia nodded. Once home, she stayed curled up in her room, half asleep, for the next three days. The ache didn't vanish, but the roar in her ears that rose whenever she thought about Abby kept the silence at bay. She talked with Gem a lot, and she texted a bit with Devon. Even Ben called to keep her company.

By the time Abby's funeral was only an hour away, Lia was trapped between a nausea-inducing dread and a sharp, stabbing fear in the back of her mind of facing the rest of her Lincoln. She had been avoiding the news and the internet. She didn't want to know what was being said.

"Hey," Gem said as they met up outside Abby's church. "You okay?"

Everything felt muffled and distant, as if Lia were watching the procession alone and drowning beneath a thin veil of water. "Don't leave me."

"Never," Gem said.

Lia managed a weak smile. Come May, everyone was leaving with plans and dreams. Everyone except Abby.

Lia sat in the back, Gem on one side and her parents on the other. People milled about, whispering to each other. The casket was closed, and Abby's parents were sequestered behind the privacy of a sheer curtain that did nothing to block the sound of them crying. Omelet's soft huffs peppered the proceedings.

Abby's mom spoke, then Georgia, and one of Abby's colleagues at the vet office where she volunteered.

Lia couldn't cry. She stared at the dark wood of Abby's coffin and kept a tight grip on Gem's hand. Most of the school had come, and Lia could feel the stares.

"I wonder why it's closed?" someone whispered behind Lia.

Someone chuckled. "I heard she cracked her head open. I bet they couldn't fix that."

"It's stupid," the other person muttered back. "A runner. Tripping. To death."

A rushing sound filled her ears. Omelet's *ah-woo* echoed through the room. Someone cracked their knuckles, bones snapping. Breaking. Like Abby's.

It hadn't been branches. It hadn't been branches. None of the sounds she'd heard that morning had been branches.

Lia leapt to her feet and ran out of the church. Her hands shook as she pushed open the doors. Her feet thudded across the marble entry hall, and she shoved her way into the cold. Lia collapsed on the top step of the stairs leading down to the street and pressed her hands against her eyes. The dark behind her eyelids was the same dark in Abby's dented head. The sunlight burned.

The door opened behind her. Two sets of footsteps stopped next to Lia. Devon and Gem.

"You're breathing too fast," Devon said. There was no judgment in his voice, and his fingers brushed her hands. "Try to control it."

Lia drew a short, shuddering breath through her nose. "How can I control it when something as simple as tripping killed her?"

"Okay, don't think about that part," Devon said.

"I need a distraction," Lia said. "I need to do something. I can't sit still. I can't stay home. I can't just think because I'll end up thinking about her. And what they're saying. If they're saying that stuff here, what are they saying at school? When they're alone?"

"They're saying they're scared," Gem told her. "They're saying they're sad. They're saying the world doesn't make sense. They're saying the game is tainted because Abby was excited about playing it and now she can't. They're sobbing in the school bathroom and needing parents to come pick them up."

Gem sat next to Lia. "They are not those two idiots who were sitting behind us."

Lia pulled her hands from her eyes and took a slow breath. "I don't have anything to do. I don't have anything to think about. They excused me from school, but I can't not think about Abby if I'm thinking about nothing. Does that make sense?"

"Sort of," Devon said. "You had a lot of *nots* in there."

"I did!" Lia sniffed and laughed, the sound ripping out of her throat until she wasn't sure why she was laughing at all but it was all she could do to keep from crying. Lia covered her mouth with her hands.

"I need something to do," she said. "I need something to fill up this space in my head or else Abby will fill it up. Talk to me about something. The game. Is anyone out?"

Devon sighed. "They were considering banning the game."

"The school isn't in charge of it," Lia said. "How could they cancel it?"

"Anyone found playing would get in-school suspension." Devon wiped Lia's cheeks with his hand and flicked a damp eyelash aside. "My mom said the PTA brought it up."

"I bet half of them were those busybodies speculating on what happened before your parents got you out of that park," Gem said. "The news even interviewed them."

Lia rubbed her nose. "I saw them when I was leaving."

"Why were you following Abby?" Devon asked. "We made a deal."

"I wanted to see what path she would take so we could set up there when the deal was done," Lia said. "I didn't want to come back and have nothing."

Gem laid their cheek against the top of Lia's head. "You want to keep playing Assassins?"

"What else do I have if I don't?" Lia asked. "Why was I even there if not?"

"I think you have a lot, but I don't think you'll listen to me when I say that," Gem said. "I'll keep playing, but no more early-morning solo runs, okay?"

Lia nodded. "I don't think I can go back in there."

"I'll tell your parents," Devon said, squeezing her hand before heading back into the church.

"Yeah, I don't blame you," Gem said once he was gone. "It was really stuffy. Not enough dogs."

"There should've been a lot more," Lia said. "Like fifteen,

minimum, and then people could've adopted them. Abby would've liked that."

"She would have," Gem said. "I know you want to keep playing the game, but please don't do anything else that could get you killed. You're my best friend, and I love you."

Lia relaxed against Gem.

"I love you, too," she said. "No more dangerous things. I promise."

CHAPTER 9

Hello, Lia Prince.
Our condolences, but if we know you as well as we
think we do, this message will be much appreciated.
Your new target is Leo Liu.
Happy hunting,
The Council

Lia and Gem waited in the main office after asking to talk to Mrs. White, the principal. When they said it was about Assassins, several of the secretaries glanced up.

It was the first time Lia had visited the principal. She sat in the principal's office on a hard wooden chair with a cushion tied to the seat, the sort of chair she normally only saw at her grandmother's dining room table, and Gem sat next to her. Mrs. White sat behind her desk, fingers laced beneath her chin.

The school hadn't made playing Assassins against the rules yet.

Some of the more vocal parents were pushing for it, though. Lia's parents had insisted she not play the game anymore. If she hadn't been playing, she wouldn't have suffered. If she hadn't been playing, maybe things would've been different. Maybe Abby would never have fallen, hurt her arm, and taken that path. Maybe she wouldn't have died.

But not playing wasn't an option.

Lia took a deep breath, held it, and tried to keep her voice steady. "I heard that you're thinking about punishing seniors who continue playing Assassins?"

"Yes, well." Mrs. White cleared her throat. "In light of Abby's accident, we are afraid that the unregulated nature of the game and how it encourages and rewards risky behavior will put more students in danger."

"She wanted to play," Gem protested. "And she definitely wouldn't have wanted to go down in history as the girl who got Assassins banned. She would hate that."

Mrs. White's mouth twitched. "I understand that it's a tradition; however, given the nature of what's happened, it feels distasteful to continue."

"It's only distasteful if we make it distasteful," Lia said before Mrs. White could continue. "We're not just saying this because we want to play. The game has never been banned, and in five years when no one who knew her is here, she'll be a joke. But if we keep playing, we can make it matter. Every time someone takes out their target, we can make a donation to the no-kill animal shelter Abby volunteered at."

Lia had asked Devon and Ben about it, and Devon had originally called her idea a "swear jar for kills" but agreed that it worked.

"That may be, but this tragedy shines a light on—"

"It was dark." Lia stared at a spot on the wall just over the principal's shoulder. "So if there's anything that needs a light, it's that park. I tripped, too. I was just lucky."

The room was silent for a moment; then Mrs. White rose and gestured for Lia and Gem to do the same.

"I appreciate you both stopping by, and I'll keep your idea in mind," Mrs. White told them, opening her door. "As of now, we haven't made any decisions. I am afraid you two need to get to class, though."

She shut the door and Gem shrugged. "Parents are scared. Mine are. Neither of them grew up in a town like Lincoln, and now all the Lincoln parents are realizing how little attention they've paid to what their kids are up to."

"That's not our fault," Lia said.

"Yeah," Gem said. "Good luck explaining that to them."

They got to class a few minutes before the tardy bell. The biology room was completely silent, and even Sam, who usually listened to music without headphones, was staring solemnly at Abby's empty chair. There was a whole block of empty desks where Abby usually sat, and Lia swallowed. At least they weren't in the lab. There were three desks between Abby and Lia. Devon had even sat in the normally unoccupied desk near Lia. His tall frame would block her view of Abby's desk.

They were supposed to be finishing up the chapters on anatomy. Ms. Christie played *Planet Earth* instead. Even Faith, who usually complained about anything that didn't go according to plan, was calmly sitting in a chair at the back of the room so that she could get a better view of the screen. She raised one hand to Lia in greeting.

"Hey," Devon said. He leaned across the aisle to slip a note card beneath her arms. "That's what the daily quiz was on for Euro History."

"Thank you," Lia whispered. Her throat still hurt from crying, but maybe he would think she was just being quiet for the movie. She slid her journal into the metal basket beneath her chair.

She tore out a page from her notebook and wrote, *Did you get the email from the Council?*

She angled it so Devon could see, and he nodded, pulling out his own sheet of paper. *Did the swear jar work?*

I don't know, wrote Lia. *In-school suspension seems pretty tame now. What is there left to lose?*

Death had never seemed real, but now it was random and un-avoidable even if you did everything adults said you should. Why bother with rules?

A bunch of people withdrew. Devon tapped his pen against the paper, dark ink splotches seeping across the white.

Abby's sweatshirt. Omelet's fur.

Four years she had waited for this. It wasn't fair.

I'm going to keep playing no matter what, she wrote. *But I under-stand if you can't.*

She glanced at him, expecting a frown or a sigh, some sort of sign that upright Devon Diaz didn't approve, but he only crum-pled up his note and tucked it into his backpack.

"I thought you might say that," he whispered. "Do you have a plan?"

"No," Lia said, sneaking a glance at her phone. She sent a quick email to the Council. "But I will soon."

CHAPTER 10

"The game is on," Gem said. It was after school and Lia and Gem were on a bench next to the parking lot. They looked at the texted screenshot on Gem's phone. "The school will punish anyone found playing the game who breaks school rules, but we don't play on school grounds anyway."

Someone had sent Gem a screenshot from the PTA Facebook group, and they hadn't bothered to cut out the names of the parents with the most to say. Lia's mom was not happy by the looks of it.

"Y'all see it?" Ben came over to the bench and held up his phone. "Look."

> Hello, assassins.
> Today we honor a fallen comrade, Abby Ascher. She was brilliant. She was bold. She will be missed. She will not be the reason the game is canceled. The game will never be canceled. The game will only end when all assassins but one are dead. The school has taken an interest in our goings-on of late, and while

we will take no part in the donations to the animal
shelter, we will not punish those who opt to. Perhaps
the promise of kindness will draw out your ambition.
That said, players and teams who have withdrawn
because they feared retribution from the school will
not be reinstated. Cowardice will not be rewarded.
Happy hunting,
The Council

"Happy hunting," Gem said. "Definitely not Gabo. He liked
Abby."

"There are fewer people playing," Lia said. "Leo must still be,
or we would have gotten a new target."

"He is. He loves a good competition." Ben crawled over the
bench and squeezed himself between Gem and Lia. "How you
doing?"

Ben was the first person who didn't ask it while looking at her
like she was dying.

"Better," Lia said. "I need something to do. The game's been all
I've been looking forward to since ninth grade. I'm ready to go."

The reminders she had—skinned knees and a thick bruise
across her ankle—were already fading.

"I love a good competition, too." Ben stretched his arms up
and twisted till his spine cracked.

Lia winced.

"Diaz!" Ben waved behind them. "We're still in. Are you?"

"He said he'd play if we wouldn't get in-school suspension,"
Lia said. "So he's in."

Devon held up his phone as he approached. "Yeah, I got your
message."

Lia turned back around, about to ask what message, and Devon winked at her. She shut her mouth. He'd never done that before.

"So what's the plan?" Ben asked.

"Lia?" Devon leaned his arms against the bench back, shoulder bumping Lia's head. "You're the stalker."

"That makes me sound creepy." Lia reached into her backpack for her journal. Her fingers scraped across cheap paper and cardboard covers, but the journal was nowhere to be found. "Shoot. I left my journal in Ms. Christie's class."

"Want to go back to get it?" Gem asked. "I don't remember seeing it when we left, but Faith was behind us. I'll text her."

Gem typed something, and a few seconds later nodded.

"Faith says she saw it when she left but forgot it was yours. Ms. Christie probably has it now."

"It's fine," Lia said. It wasn't fine. She had spent months working on it, and Leo's data was in there. "I have most of it online, and my name and email are in the journal. Ms. Christie won't toss it. Let's just focus on Leo."

"Leo Liu," Devon said, peering over Lia's shoulder and reading from her phone. "Soccer star, best history student, vegetarian."

"He makes great lentil burgers," Ben said, leaning forward. "He has practice tonight if we want to get him. Afterward he'll be with the other players. They carpool."

"I have a family dinner tonight," Devon said. "Are you good if I catch back up with you tomorrow?"

Her skin prickled at the brush of his breath past her ear. "Sure. Just make sure you don't go anywhere alone."

From the corner of her eye, Lia saw Gem wink at her.

"Yeah, yeah." He smiled. "If I need anyone to accompany me anywhere, I'll message you."

"I can't do tonight either," Gem said, "but I can drop everyone off to make sure none of us get taken out."

Lia couldn't stomach referring to the targets as "killed," and was glad they'd used "taken out." "Ben and I can see if we can get Leo tonight, and then we can regroup tomorrow if not?"

"Yes." Ben clapped Gem on the back and pulled his hood over his red hair. "Think you'll survive if you drive home alone?"

Gem hummed and stood. "Yeah, unless they break into my garage."

Technically illegal, so they were probably safe.

Gem drove Devon home first. They pulled onto his street as his mother was getting home, Dr. Diaz lingering at the door. Lia hadn't seen her at the funeral, but she couldn't remember much of that day anyway. She waved to them.

"She's anxious because of Abby," Gem said softly. "My parents are, too. I can't believe yours aren't, Lia."

They were. They were worried about her taking too much time off school even while telling her she needed to focus on her health. They wanted her to recover and take as much time off as she needed. They wanted her to keep her grades up. They wanted a daughter they could be proud of.

They wanted so much for her, all of it without asking what she wanted.

They had never even let her take off school if she was sick in the past. She couldn't believe it would really be okay if she needed more time off now.

"Ben," Lia said, turning to look at him, "are your parents okay with you being out late?"

He nodded. "As long as I text them where I am and am home by ten."

"I promise to get you home for dinner." Lia smiled. "Gem, drop us off at the soccer fields."

"No." Ben pulled up his phone, squinted, and shook his head. "Drop us at that 7-Eleven near them. It's uphill. We can watch from there."

They grabbed snacks from the store after Gem dropped them off. Ben piled all of it into his backpack and led Lia to a small, tree-filled alley overlooking the soccer fields. There were several well-worn dirt paths cutting through.

"How'd you know this was up here?" Lia asked, settling down with her back to a tree.

He sat next to her and pointed to a clearer area barely large enough to hide a car. "My ex and I used to come here."

"Cool," Lia said quickly. "What do you know about Leo?"

"Enough." Ben laughed. "He's dating Ryan, and they're on a team together. I'm guessing Shane and Carlos are the other two on the team. They're all faster than you, so don't chase them. Ryan and Carlos are definitely faster than you and probably faster than me. We'll have to catch Leo when he thinks he's safe. Maybe at the gym? He's more an endurance guy, usually at the back during their post-workout lap. I bet we could separate him from the pack."

"Yeah, maybe. They run around the gym, right? I don't know what to do with that," Lia said. Two weeks ago, she would've lured him off the path or rolled something before him to make him stop, but now she couldn't stomach the idea. "Why don't you play soccer? You did when we were kids, and then you swapped to football."

Ben offered her some pretzels. "I don't know. May's better at soccer. Didn't want to make our dads pick which game to go to, and now our games are different nights."

"I think my mom would be happier if I played a sport," Lia said, taking a pretzel and breaking it at the joints. "If I'm not good at school, I might as well be good at a sport."

"Didn't your brother play basketball?" Ben asked.

Lia nodded. "Since he was five. I don't like it, though."

"Yeah, but you did debate and stuff," he said. "Don't those count?"

"Only if I want to go to law school, apparently. Since I don't, my parents don't think debate's very useful," Lia said. "They figured it was a distraction, so I quit to focus on grades."

That hadn't worked, and now she had the same grades and no debate club. She pulled the binoculars up to her eyes and watched Leo take a water break with some other players. What was the point of her parents paying and helping with loans if she didn't have a plan? According to them, there wasn't one. She had plans for Assassins and escape rooms, but not a single one for life after graduation.

It infuriated her parents.

Footsteps pattered across the ground behind them, and Lia glanced over her shoulder. Leaves fluttered to the ground. Nothing was there.

Ben patted her shoulder. "Probably Slushie, but I get it. I've been hearing stuff, too. Or at least imagining it. Last night I nearly punched a tree. Thought it was attacking me in the backyard. I could've sworn there was a person behind it, but nope. Nothing but trees."

"Slushie?" she repeated, confused.

"Slushie," he confirmed, and took the binoculars from her. "The 7-Eleven's cat."

He said it with such certainty that Lia could only nod. They watched the practice carry on in silence, and when the sun got low and the players ran one last sprint and called it a night, Lia took note of which car Leo got into and entered it on her phone. Ben said it was Ryan's.

"So he's almost certainly on a team with Ryan, Carlos, and Shane," Lia said, lowering the binoculars. All three of them were driving home together. "Where do you think he's going now?" Lia asked.

"Babysitting," Ben said. He tipped the pretzel bag up and emptied the crumbs into his mouth. "He's CPR certified and everything."

"We can't get him tonight," Lia said, biting into a chocolate bar. "But we can get him tomorrow."

CHAPTER 11

The next morning, Lia rose with the sun and Abby didn't. The fact haunted her, a ghost at her heels as she packed her bag for a Saturday of assassinating Leo. She had spent all night figuring out how to get Leo, and the thrill of the game, of doing something right, lifted the weight in the pit of her stomach. She waited in the dark of her living room for Gem, the sounds of her father's snoring thundering in her ears. Maybe if she won, she would feel better about having been the one who lived.

"Survivor's guilt," Gem said as Lia got into the backseat next to Devon and told them how she was feeling. "We talked about it in psych once."

"Cool," Lia said, because putting a name to it didn't really help. "So, about Leo—the team has to cross the street when they do their lap around the grounds. That means they have to wait for the light, and they usually go in two or three groups. Leo's usually last, and when everyone crosses the street, there's a stretch of sidewalk that's usually blocked by traffic. He'll feel safe. He won't speed up because usually he wouldn't be alone. We hit the crosswalk buttons on either end of the street and delay traffic, and one of us takes him out while he's crossing that stretch. He won't be in the line of sight of the others if they all stick to their usual running patterns, and given how exhausting practice is, they probably will."

"On top of things as always," Devon said.

"Gem and Ben will hit the crosswalk buttons. Because of traffic, they won't count as alone, so we have to stop traffic," Lia said. "Devon or I will take the shot from across the drainage ditch."

"Going to challenge me to a duel to determine who the best shot is?" Devon asked.

Lia grinned. "I'm the best shot. I was just going to let you take it if you wanted."

The best gym in Lincoln was across from a closed YMCA. Gem let Devon and Lia off in the YMCA's parking lot, all three making sure no cars had followed them and no one was watching from the windows of the gym. Devon helped Lia out of the car and flipped up his hood. If they got caught, it would be best if Leo didn't know it was them. She pulled her wool hat lower.

"Here," she said, and pointed to the gate at the edge of the overgrown YMCA lot. There was no fence attached to it, and the little valley behind it was meant for water runoff, but it had been far too dry for that. "It's not trespassing; I checked. We can keep watch from atop the other side. The moment Leo's alone, we've got him."

"How many times did you spy on the team to figure this out?" Devon asked, his face drenched in light from the rising sun.

"Only a few times," she said, not meeting his eyes. "It meant I knew enough about the whole team to call it there."

He shook his head, and Lia trudged out of the creek and up

into the little forested area separating the neighborhood from the old lot. His chuckling followed her.

"What?" she asked. "Not all of us have everything figured out. I need something to be good at, and games are it. Competitions. You've got orchestra, and I've got this."

Lia had always needed something. She was hungry, but everyone always told her that what she wanted wasn't right. It was like wanting bread and being told carbs were bad. She wanted to do what she wanted, and here she was, finally doing it, except none of it was right.

Devon squeezed his eyes shut and sat on a mossy rock. "I'm worried about you."

"Oh," Lia said. "Don't be. I'm fine."

He stared at her.

"I'm mostly fine." She shrugged. "I need something to do. I don't have anything else to think about except sad things—Abby and graduation and Mark—and I want to do something good. I want to finally be the best at something."

Devon cleared the dirt off the rock next to him. "Come here."

"Why?" She sat next to him, a not-uncomfortable shudder in her spine. "What's wrong?"

"If you keep standing," he said, "Leo will see you."

Lia grinned. "Thank you. And now we wait," she said.

After the first five minutes, Devon slouched. His shoulder rested against hers, and she pulled her binoculars from their case, cleaning a smudge from the lens. He didn't bring up his feelings on the game again, and Lia didn't push her luck. It figured that he hated it and thought she had bad taste. That was the implication, anyway.

She hated implications. They kept her up at night, reminding her of all the missteps she had ever taken. She had always hoped he at least liked her as a person.

"Lia," he whispered suddenly, "I think I—"

Her phone vibrated, and he shook his head.

"He's on his last lap and last in the pack," Lia said, reading Gem's text. "Stopping traffic now."

Lia rose to her knees on the rock. Devon braced against her side, keeping her steady. The stragglers ran past, and a single figure bringing up the rear came into sight. Leo slowed a bit, shaking out his ankle, and glanced up and down the street. The runners ahead of him turned the corner. He froze.

Lia pulled the trigger, and water splattered against Leo's chest. He stumbled back and shrieked. Lia leapt to her feet.

"Yes!" Her water gun hit the ground, and she grabbed the towel from her bag. "Leo, you are officially out."

He stared up at her, mouth a wide O.

"The hell, Prince?" he shouted, and laughed. "Did you clear the road or something? How long have you been back there?"

"Not long. Sorry, but you're out," Lia said, tossing him the towel. "No hard feelings?"

"Man, I hope the rest of my team gets you next." But Leo snorted as he said it and threw the towel at her. "Solid, though. I didn't think anyone would just wait around on the off chance I'd be alone for a few seconds. Am I your first?"

Lia nodded.

"I got to get back," Leo said after a minute of laughing and drying off. "Nice shot."

"Thanks."

The moment Leo vanished over the edge of the creek, Devon

wrapped Lia in a hug. His arms pinned hers to her side, and his hands clutched the back of her coat. Lia froze, nose to his shoulder and heart in her throat, and he squeezed her once. His breath ruffled her hair.

"Your plan worked," he said. "You were right."

He let her go as quickly as he had grabbed her, and Lia could only pat his shoulder. "We did it."

"You did it," he said, following her out of the creek. "I just watched."

"Still, I like having you around." She laughed and shook her head. "It's just a game, but it makes me happy."

Tires squealed in the distance. Lia jerked, twisting toward where the sound had come from. Branches bobbed in the forest, each rustle and creak another shock to her heart, and a shadow that might have been a car driving past slipped through the trees. Devon's fingers tightened around hers, and he tugged her toward the gym parking lot.

"You're not alone," he said. "If you see your assassin, they can't kill you now."

"I don't see anyone. I keep thinking I do. I thought—" She glanced down. Her hands were shaking. She couldn't feel them at all. She pressed her scabbed palms together and hissed. "I thought I saw someone that morning with Abby. I didn't."

"The game and Abby, even though it was an accident, are making you paranoid." His fingers brushed her back and fell away. "That's why I'm worried."

She waved to Gem across the street. "Maybe it is just that. Have you noticed anyone following you?"

He shook his head. "Like I told you before, I haven't noticed anything out of the ordinary."

She was pretty sure he hadn't told her before, but she *had* forgotten nearly a whole day and her journal.

"Maybe your assassin hasn't gotten serious yet," Lia said, "or they got taken out already."

"Maybe," he said. "Still a pity I don't get to take you out."

"If we're the last team standing, then you can take me out."

She froze.

"Is that a promise?" he asked, glancing at her from the corner of his eye.

"Threat." Lia smiled, full of their success against Leo and her need for something better than what her life was right then, and said, "If we're the last team standing, you can *try* to take me out."

CHAPTER 12

Their new target was a kid Lia knew only by voice. Peter Baird had been reading the announcements since they were freshmen, his ever-happy voice a staticky constant, and Lia had only ever seen him from across hallways. She had been sure he wouldn't play since he never seemed to do anything except read the announcements and go to class, but to be fair, all she ever did was go to class. It would be hard to get him.

Devon had returned to his usual seat in biology, though he had dropped a note on Lia's desk before class started. He was being followed; his assassin was shorter than him, which didn't narrow the options down; and orchestra rehearsals for the spring concert were starting Wednesday. Lia drew an *X* over her quick scribble of Peter's class schedule. She couldn't find any times during the week when Peter would be alone.

"Group work time." Gem knocked on Lia's desk, dragging Lia out of her desk and pulling their seats to connect with Devon's. "You two good with this?"

Devon nodded. His neighbor and default group partner, Faith, scooted her desk back. Ms. Christie passed out a packet of problems.

"What are we doing?" Lia asked Gem softly.

"Proving Hess's law," Gem whispered. "Biochemistry, chapter thirty-two."

"Here," said Faith, handing over a full page of perfectly ordered notes that were color-coded and highlighted. Her looping cursive was beautiful and impossible to read. "I'm glad you're back at school. How are you?"

"I'm fine," Lia said on instinct. "Just a bit distracted. Thank you."

"No problem." Faith flipped open her packet, fingers tapping at the edge of her desk, and signed her name at the top. "Did they tell you anything about what happened? I can't believe she tripped."

"Faith," muttered Devon. "Don't."

"Sorry," she said quickly.

"She tripped." Lia filled out her name at the top of the worksheet. It was chicken scratch in comparison to Faith's. "And landed wrong."

Faith hummed. They passed the packet around and filled out the ones they knew off the tops of their heads. Gem and Faith made small talk, and Lia slipped Devon the schedule she had written down of Peter's, a little asterisk next to his after-school activities.

"Do you know Peter?" Lia asked Faith after they had exhausted their knowledge of biology and had resorted to flipping through their book for help. "He's our next target."

"He arrives fifteen minutes early to read the announcements, gets to class ten minutes late, and is in all regular classes plus creative writing," said Faith. "That's all I know."

That was all Lia knew, too, and all she had written in her journal. Ms. Christie didn't have it, and Lia knew that meant it had been tossed by the janitor. A year she had spent on that journal, and now it was covered in ham cubes and misprinted exams at the bottom of a Dumpster.

Lia flipped to the back of her school agenda and wrote *Abby Ascher* in the neatest script she could. After the name, she added a single tick mark. At least winning meant they were doing something good for the shelter, too.

Gem flipped through their book and groaned. "Which of you knows how to do problem eighteen?" they asked. "It's the only one we haven't got."

"Yeah, one sec," said Faith. She dug into her backpack and pulled out a crinkled packet of papers identical to the one they were working on. "My sister had Ms. Christie, too. This is easier."

Devon pulled the packet onto his desk and studied question eighteen. "That seems slightly against the rules."

"It's homework, not a test," said Faith. "In the real world, you can look up formulas. Look, I even alphabetized her notes and assignments. Flip to *H*."

Gem spun their pen along the back of their knuckles and tapped a page in their book. "Don't bother. I got it."

"Work smarter," Faith said. "Not harder."

The group finished the packet with twenty minutes to spare. Ms. Christie was busy trying not to chide Georgia for reading, and the others were quietly chatting. Devon read over Peter's schedule.

"He'll be at several orchestra rehearsals, you know," Devon

said. "He's always the announcer at concerts and plays. The house has him record everything the week before dress rehearsals so that he doesn't have to be there every night."

"I've never gone to a concert," Gem said.

"No," Devon said, "you haven't."

"Shut up," Gem said. "Lia doesn't go either."

"She went to the first few." Devon looked over Gem's work on question eighteen and set the packet aside. "You sat in the back, and then you walked out during one of my solos and stopped coming altogether."

Lia looked up. She'd gone to the concerts hoping something might happen with Devon. "You remember that?"

"Of course," he said, as if it were nothing at all. That was the danger with Devon Diaz—she was never quite sure when he was being sincere or sarcastic. "Are you the only one allowed to notice people?"

"No," she said, "but you've never mentioned that."

"You've never really talked to me," Devon said, smiling. "Anyway, it was the height of rudeness, and I've hated you ever since. It's why I joined Assassins in the first place."

Faith rolled her eyes and powered on her phone, hiding the light of the iPhone under her desk. "Again. Shocked you're playing."

"School's almost over. What do I have to live for now if not revenge?" He shrugged. "Not as weird as you starting CrossFit."

"God, you're so much more sarcastic than I thought," Gem said. "I can't believe you wasted four years not talking to anyone but band kids."

"Band and orchestra aren't the same thing," he clarified. "Also, that's rich coming from a theater kid."

"Why *are* you in theater?" Faith asked, turning to give Gem a once-over. "You're top of the class, diverse, perfect for law school. Theater's like the one weird spot on your college apps."

Gem shrugged. "I like theater. I like getting to lord my power over the props table. I like messing around with the squibs," Gem said. "They don't usually call me 'diverse' either, so that's a plus."

Faith flushed. "Sorry. I'm so sorry. I—"

"We know," Lia said.

Devon cut in. "Can I borrow your pen, Gem?"

"Oh, sure," Gem said, and reached into their bag. "Here."

Gem held out the pen in a flat palm and pushed it up their sleeve to their elbow. Devon reached for the pen, slowly, and Gem lifted their pinkie and brought it down. The pen flipped out of their hand and under it. Gem turned their hand over. No pen.

Devon laughed.

"When did you learn magic?" Faith asked.

Gem had started practicing sleight of hand after a particularly intense middle school version of *Robin Hood,* and mostly did stage work now—props, sets, and front-of-house manager. Last semester's rendition of *Wait Until Dark* had left Gem exhausted and up to their elbows in fake blood and prop knives.

"Magic's not real," Gem said. "I'm just impressive. If you ever went to a play, you would know that."

Later, when school was over, Lia met up with Gem in the parking lot.

"I'm sorry about earlier," Gem said. "You've seen my tricks so often."

"I never get tired of it," Lia said, wrapping one arm around Gem's waist. "Never. Except that one with the fake blood. Don't do that one again without warning me. Took ages to get the stain out."

Gem unlocked the car doors and they both got in.

They leaned their head against the steering wheel. "I know we have things to do, but can one of the things be a nap?"

"After we follow Peter to wherever he goes at night," Lia said, patting Gem's back.

Gem groaned. Lia laughed and let her head fall against the window. Outside, a figure stood at the open trunk of a car across the lot with their face turned to Gem and Lia. Lia raised a hand to block her reflection, and Gem started the car. The figure tossed something heavy into the trunk and slammed it shut.

"I think we're being followed," Lia said.

Gem sighed. "This is fun, but I'll be glad when it's done. Let them follow. We can take them."

The car—a small blue hatchback—followed them for five minutes before turning off into a Sonic. Lia couldn't quite make out the driver's face, and Gem kept two cars behind Peter, who hadn't seemed to notice he was being followed. He immediately went home, and for two hours went nowhere else. Gem and Lia did homework in the car, peeking down the street every few minutes to make sure Peter didn't leave. He didn't.

Finally Gem and Lia called it a night, and Lia decided to follow him in the morning.

"You'll be on your own," Gem said. "I am going to the gym."

Lia scrunched up her nose. "You never go to the gym."

"It's a new thing I'm trying," Gem said, blushing. "May's going with me."

"Really? That's great!" Lia said. Sometimes she had to remind herself that people led lives outside the game. She just wasn't able to be one of them.

After Gem dropped her off, she stood there, in the entry hall, alone. It was nearly eight. Dinner was little more than the slightly charred scent of Brussels sprouts—they'd stopped having family dinners after Mark went to college since they couldn't do family dinners without the whole family.

"Lia?" her mom called. The music in the kitchen lowered. "That you?"

"Yeah! I was with Gem."

"Did you get your homework done?" Her mom came around the corner, familiar tense face. "What's wrong?"

"Nothing," Lia said quickly. She had already witnessed a murder and dragged her family through that. She was fine. She was. She needed to keep moving. "Just thinking. Can I eat?"

"Of course." Her mom shot her an odd look and headed back toward the kitchen. "Come on. I'll warm up the chicken."

Lia's phone vibrated in her pocket, and she fished it out. Devon had texted her:

> Peter started birdwatching after New Year's, and I bet he meets up with that club.

> My mom can drop me off at your house and we can walk. I'll bring breakfast. You bring binoculars.

And the game was on.

CHAPTER 13

Lia wasn't sure how Devon knew where she lived. She opened the door before he could knock, slipping out into the dark with him. The morning was cold, colder than it usually was in March, and the wind ripped through their coats like shears through paper. Devon was bundled up in a black wool coat and burgundy scarf, and his hair was curled from the wind. He clutched a small white bag in his left hand, and Lia stayed on his right. Despite the chill, she kept a few inches between them. If Devon wasn't interested in dating, she shouldn't push it.

"You cold?" he asked, and pulled his right hand from his pocket. "Here."

He held out his hand and Lia took it. He tucked her hand into his pocket. At the bottom was one of those hot packets that stayed warm after snapping, and he closed her fingers around it. Lia crossed her other arm over her chest and shoved it under her arm. Devon's fingers curled around her hand.

"Thank you," Lia said, ducking her head against the wind and hoping the cold hid her warm cheeks. "So Peter bird-watches? Even on days like this?"

"Especially on ones like this." He squeezed her hand. "It's a matter of pride, I think? I don't know. He likes birds."

It was a while to the park, and Lia's parents had agreed to let her walk there since Devon was with her. The dark, though, closed in. The silence made the back of her neck itch.

"Stop." Devon stopped at the edge of a small parking lot, a lush green park full of frost-ridden evergreens and a trail lined with rosemary bushes leading into the dark. The sun was peeking over the horizon, and he untangled his hand from hers. "We have about fifteen minutes before they show up. Some kid leads it. He's trying to make it a thing."

"How do you know?"

He handed her the white bag. "If I tell you I tried it last year, how much will you laugh?"

Lia grinned.

"I hated it," he said. "Here. You like cinnamon rolls, right?"

"They're my favorite," she said, following him into the park. "For this, I won't laugh."

"How kind of you," Devon said, and he hid his smile behind a hand.

They settled into a little thicket far off the trail but close enough to watch Peter arrive. The light filtered through the trees and barely lit their little spot. Devon walked behind a large tree trunk, and the branches rustled. Somewhere, far off, a dog barked. Lia froze.

"Lia?" Devon asked. "You okay?"

She had been so sure in that second that he would be bloody and dying. There would be a crash. She would find him dead.

"Yeah," she said, sitting on an old railroad tie next to him. "Sorry."

"It's okay. Go ahead and eat," he said. "We're together, so we're safe."

Lia laughed and smiled. "My brave assassin shield."

"I'm just glad you finally started talking to me again." He opened the bag and pulled out a cinnamon roll larger than his hand. "We've got five minutes. They really just congregate and stare at trees while two country club guys talk about this one time they saw an ivory-billed woodpecker."

Lia pulled out her cinnamon roll. It was still hot and gooey, the cinnamon filling laced with chopped walnuts and pecans. The first bird-watcher showed up with a car full of kids when Lia was halfway done with her roll, and Devon ducked down with her behind the bushes. He shoved the last handful of his roll into his mouth and cleaned up with hand sanitizer. Peter arrived second, stepping out into the cold with a puff of warm breath. The crowd grew to fifteen over the next five minutes.

"I bet he always arrives second," muttered Devon with cinnamon clinging to his lips and cheek. "He likes to arrive places on the hour."

"Devon, wait," she whispered, and wiped the cinnamon sugar from the corner of his mouth with her thumb. "There."

His lips parted slightly. His face tilted to hers. "Lia?"

"Assassins with cinnamon on their lips aren't scary." She let her hand linger on his cheek. "You're ready now."

Lia downloaded a map of the trails. Peter was at the start of the group, alone and red-cheeked. Devon and Lia followed them for a minute to check which path they took at a fork and then returned to their seats, where they could see the end of the trail. The bird-watchers returned in small groups with thermoses and cameras clasped in their hands. Peter wasn't last but he was close. Devon narrowed his eyes as Peter left. The other person who had arrived first stayed until everyone was gone. They stretched near their car.

"Wait here," Lia said.

Nothing could happen to him when they were only a few feet apart.

Lia crept forward to see who it was. She stayed low and darted through the trees to the other side of the lot. She pushed some branches aside. The guy in charge wasn't old at all; he was an alum from Mark's year. She couldn't remember his name, but she knew where he lived. Mark had made her wait in the car often enough when stopping by his house. He left after a few minutes. She turned back to Devon.

A shadow stood in the foliage behind him. It raised an arm, something dark grasped in its hands. Lia darted back, ripping her own water gun out in a blink, and fired one shot. It splattered against the trees, and she tackled Devon. His back hit the forest floor, her body slamming into his chest. The shadow fled deeper into the park.

"So," Devon said. His lashes brushed her cheek and his words warmed her ear. One of his hands curled around her hip. "I guess someone is trying to take me out."

CHAPTER 14

By the time they walked back to Lia's house, Lia's blush was mostly replaced by frostbite. Devon kept her close, though, insisting they share his pocket warmer again. Lia couldn't complain. She couldn't say much of anything without stuttering.

"So Gem's picking us up?" Devon asked.

Lia nodded.

Devon ran a hand through his dark hair. "Do you want to meet at the same time tomorrow? I can bring breakfast again."

"You don't have to," Lia said.

"I want to. We can try to get Peter and maybe whoever is after me."

Lia nodded and waved to Gem, who had just pulled up. "Deal."

When they got to school, Devon hopped out of the car and took off for orchestra. Gem turned to Lia.

"May is amazing," Gem said, a hitch in their breath.

Lia laughed. "But most importantly, can she bench-press you?"

"She hasn't yet, but she definitely could." Gem collapsed over the steering wheel. "She was so nice, too. She waited to make sure

I knew how to do everything and brought me water. She even had snacks."

"Cute," Lia said. "I'm glad."

There was a glow in Gem's cheeks. "How was your breakfast date?"

"It wasn't a date," Lia said. "I think we can get Peter Wednesday morning if we're careful. We have to delay someone. Let the air out of their tires, maybe?"

"Nope," Gem said. "Bad plan. Can't we just block the road instead?"

Lia snapped her fingers. "Way better. I'll text the others."

"Speaking of," Gem said, and pointed to Ben stalking toward the car. "What's up with him?"

"No clue," Lia said, and unlocked the doors. "Ben?"

"I'm out!" He threw his backpack into the backseat and slammed his whole body inside as if the car were a bed, not a giant box made of metal and sharp plastic. He held up one hand. "Katie Rogers got me last night. Shot my hand from twenty feet away, that beast."

He lay down face-first on the seat. Lia reached back and yanked Ben all the way into the car, and Gem shut the door. Ben at least helped a bit, not going totally limp. Lia patted the back of his knee.

"How'd she get you?" Lia asked.

"Luck," he mumbled into the cushions. "I got locked out of the house, and she got me while I was hopping the fence to get the extra key."

"I know what might cheer you up," Gem said. "You want to hear how we're going to avenge you and get Peter?"

"Hell yes." Ben sat up, eyes wide and red hair sticking up in every direction. "I can't help, but I can make sure none of y'all are alone till we win."

"Peter gets there a little early for his bird-watching thing, just a little after the main guy. Gem will block that guy in their driveway and delay him by five to ten minutes," Lia said. She looked at Gem and waited for them to nod. "We can take him out when he arrives alone and his leader isn't there."

She had no idea what master bird-watchers were called.

"Sounds good," Ben said. "You text me if you need an escort. Any day, any time. Got it?"

"Thank you," Lia said. "You're a lifesaver, and I'm sorry you're out."

"Don't worry about it," he said. "I'm only annoyed."

All day at school, she thought about the game. And by the end of the day, she was starving. She and Gem drove to a nearby takeout place.

"Would your parents mind if you called out sick to school?" Gem asked as they drove.

"They might," Lia said, lowering her seat all the way back until she was flat on her back and staring at the ceiling.

They had told her she could take more time off in that tone of "Is that what you really want to do?" that they reserved for when she was making bad decisions.

"I don't get them," Gem said. "You're not a genius, but you always do what they ask and never get in trouble."

Lia sighed. It felt wrong to complain when her life wasn't bad. Sometimes all the little things they said tangled up in Lia's chest and ached. It wasn't like she could tell someone, "Hi, my parents keep doing small things that sort of hurt my feelings. No, they never do anything really bad. They just make me feel bad." She would be laughed away.

"They should've stopped at Mark," Lia mumbled.

"Shut up." Gem got out of the car, kicking their door shut.

Lia groaned and opened the car door. A girl in a red coat pulled a large water gun from her car trunk. It was Mallory McCarty.

Popularity was a thing at Lincoln High, but they'd all known each other since kindergarten and could remember who ate boogers or peed their pants. It was hard to get too high and mighty when everyone had seen you cry because the green-colored pencil was too sharp, which had only happened to Lia once. Everyone had a story like that, except Mallory. She was pretty and had never so much as eaten glue when they were in elementary school.

And Lia had followed her for a week straight to make sure she knew her schedule in case she was Lia's target.

"Gem!" Lia called, but Gem didn't hear her.

Mallory raised the water gun and fired. Lia threw herself out of the car and tackled Gem. They tumbled to the concrete.

"Prince," Mallory said, shaking her head. "I didn't see you."

"It's okay," Lia said. She was used to it.

Gem struggled to their knees. "That scared the crap out of me."

"Sorry," Lia said, "but you almost got tagged out."

"No, I don't think that would've counted," Mallory said. Her navy lipstick, so cool against her warm brown skin, was starting to wear. "You're a witness and now you both know I'm after Gem."

Mallory helped Gem and Lia to their feet.

"I cannot believe you dove like that," Mallory told Lia. "It was really impressive."

"Thanks. That was a great shot." Lia's heart was racing in a good way, the beat a drum in her ears, and she wanted to feel this alive forever. "Did you practice? You were so far away."

"I did!" Mallory laughed.

"Great," muttered Gem. "Next time you get tackled, see if you say that after."

Mallory laughed and waved goodbye, running to a car parked on the side street. The three girls inside were laughing so hard it took them a minute to unlock the doors. Gem waved to them all.

"That was close," Gem said, wincing. "I need fifty chicken tenders."

"Let's start with five," Lia said, grabbing her phone from the car. "Weird. My phone's unlocked. No wonder it's almost dead."

CHAPTER 15

It was settled. Ben could no longer help with any assassinations now that he was out, so Gem would delay Aaron, the leader of the bird-watching club, from the safety of their car while Lia and Devon waited for Peter at the park.

Lia woke up an hour early, trying on three outfits before settling on dark jeans and a thick green sweater. She tugged at her hair, finally settling on a braid. Her mom watched from the hallway.

"Do you have waterproof mascara?" Lia asked.

"It's all a bit morbid," Lia's mom said with a yawn. "Are you sure—"

"—that I want to do the thing I woke up at four to do? Yes," Lia said. "Mascara?"

"You don't need it. It's school, not meeting the queen," her mom said. "I cannot understand your obsession with this game. If your European History exam next week is lower than eighty-five, you're not continuing."

Of course she didn't understand.

Lia pulled a hat down over her brown hair, straightened the

strands coming undone from the braid, and checked her phone. "School's basically over. Every grade that matters already happened."

Her mom sighed. "Only quitters think like that."

"It'll be fine." Lia darted past her mom. "He's here."

No makeup, no job, no dating—she couldn't have a life of her own at all. "School is your job," her parents always said, but it echoed in her mind whenever she heard them follow up with, "When you have your own money, you can spend it how you want." Everything was for her own good. She couldn't argue with that.

"If you say so," her mom muttered, peeking out at Devon through the blinds. "You have your Mace?"

"Yes."

"Keys?"

"Yes."

"Phone?"

"I've never forgotten anything before," Lia said. "Why would I now?"

Her mom only shook her head and wrapped a scarf around Lia's neck. "Text me when you get to school."

Lia opened the door before Devon could knock. He smiled and waved to her mom. Lia glared at her over her shoulder. Her mom was already gone.

"Is she really okay with you running around so early?" he asked, shifting the bag in his arms from hand to hand. "Should I introduce myself to her or something?"

"She's not really okay with anything I do, but my dad says we have to show the world we're not afraid when bad things happen," Lia said. "Like the world cares."

Devon raised his eyebrows but didn't say anything. The wind had whipped his hair into a knot at the back of his neck and chapped the tip of his nose. It wasn't cold, not even close to freezing, but the wind was wicked.

"Here." Lia unwound her scarf from her neck and wrapped it around Devon's, her fingers brushing through the ends of his hair. "Repayment for Tuesday."

"You don't owe me anything," he said softly.

They walked to the park in silence and tucked themselves into a bush closer to the lot. Lia laid her water gun in her lap. Breakfast was homemade biscuits with skillet-fried ham and hot sauce in an old plastic to-go container. He had even brought two paper towels.

They had finished eating by the time Peter rolled into the lot.

He glanced around before getting out of his car. Lia couldn't get a clear shot without standing, but Peter would see her then. Devon lobbed a rock in the opposite direction. Peter's head ripped around.

Lia leapt to her feet and fired. Water splattered against Peter's back. He shrieked, falling back against his car. His hands grasped at this side.

"What the hell!" Peter spun. "Lia Prince?"

Lia couldn't help it. She grinned, savoring the moment. "I'm sorry that you're wet now, but you're out."

Peter groaned, folded his arms on his car, and laid his head on them. "I can't believe you're even playing, Devon."

"Yeah," Devon said, "I got talked into it."

"I appealed to his need to prove me wrong," Lia said.

"It backfired." Devon peeked into Peter's backseat. "You need a dry shirt?"

"No, it's fine." Peter pushed himself up and pulled out his phone. "Let's get this over with."

As they were waiting for the Council's response, Aaron pulled into the lot. Lia had gone through three yearbooks before figuring out his name. He got out of his car and looked the trio over, chuckling as he approached. His eyes lit up when they landed on Lia.

"You out, Peter?" he asked.

Peter nodded, and Aaron ruffled his hair. Peter patted it down, white cheeks red. He scowled.

"Of course you are. Her brother Mark nearly won, so you didn't stand a chance." Aaron nodded to Lia. "Did he give you the maps he made? He knew his way through every backyard and park that year."

"No," she said. "I'm going to win on my own."

● ●

Hello, Lia.
Your contribution to our death toll has been noted,
and your new target will be provided before midnight
tomorrow. Until then, relax. But not too much.
There's still a team out to get you.
The Council

● ●

The sun had risen higher now and chased away the chill, but the wind still tore through Lia and Devon as they walked back to her house. Devon stayed close to her, his keys jangling in his pocket.

Devon shifted his shoulders. "So, you really didn't stalk me?"

"You weren't going to play, so no," she said. "It would've been a waste of time."

"Small blessings." He looped their arms together. "What's your real reason?"

"Fine. You found me out," she said. "I didn't follow you because I didn't want to be bored."

"Bold of you to insult someone who was in your middle-school classes," Devon said. "I remember when you believed the ocean was blue because it reflected the sky."

Lia wanted to lie down and sink into the earth. "She was our teacher! They're not supposed to lie!"

"She was joking." Devon laughed softly.

"They're blue for the same reason. It's all wavelengths," Lia said. "It's not my fault you're so distrusting of teachers."

"I'm distrusting of people who use their sarcasm voice constantly," Devon said. "She was mean. I can't believe she didn't count that right on the quiz when she said it in class. It wasn't your fault you thought she was serious."

"My dad said it was a good learning experience." Lia exhaled loudly.

"Did he tell you to toughen up after Abby died?" Devon cracked his neck. "Sorry. Sorry. We don't have to talk about this."

"It's okay." Lia sniffed. "Why did you really enter the game?"

He turned his face away from her, toward the sun. The light cast long shadows across his face, shadowing his deep-set eyes and highlighting the angles of his cheeks. "I don't know. Seemed fun."

"Yeah," Lia said, "but you never do anything for fun."

"Hey!" Devon rounded on her, his arm still holding hers to his side, and shot her an exaggerated frown. "I have fun."

"I've never seen it," Lia said.

She would've stuck her nose in the air, but it would've only looked like she was staring up at him. Instead, she tucked her hand into her pocket. She walked next to him, flush against his side. Devon nudged her.

"If nothing else," he said, "this is a good excuse to spend time with you."

CHAPTER 16

We should celebrate, Ben said in their group chat that night.

He'd been thrilled by the message that Peter was taken out. It was another ten bucks for Abby's shelter and a bit of revenge for him having been taken out.

We have exams coming up, Gem reminded them.

If we party at my house, May will be here, Ben said.

Gem's reply was instant. We should celebrate

We're second-semester seniors. My parents will be out of town Saturday night. We should party, Ben said.

When you say party, what do you mean exactly? Devon asked.

Parties were not really Lia's thing or, she suspected, Devon's.

Junk food, games, and whatever else we feel like, Ben said. No one can stay past midnight, and no one can get messed up. If anyone does, May and I lose guesthouse privileges

Everyone was cool with those rules.

Good. Get there whenever after five, Ben said. Bring anything you want but I'll get pizza and drinks. Also, if you got any games you want to play, bring them

By the time Lia cleared it with her parents—she told them it was a study group over dinner—Gem had sent back one message just to her.

Guest. House. Privileges.

It was hard to miss that Ben's family had money. His parents did tech stuff, giving them enough to live in Chenaux. The neighborhood was newer than its name implied, and the houses were a hodgepodge of McMansions and geometric modern things. Ben's house was one of those modern homes that looked like an Escher painting if you stared too long.

Gem picked up Lia, Devon already in the back, and Lia slid into the seat next to him. He was wearing what he always wore, though he picked at the hem of his sweater in a way Lia had never seen. Gem wore a pair of faux leather bike shorts and their mom's old University of Arkansas sweatshirt. Lia pulled her jacket tighter around her plain shirt.

"May is going to be there for a little while," Gem said instead of greeting her.

Lia glanced at Devon. "Gem has been planning their first date with May for a while now."

"It's not a date," muttered Gem, checking their reflection in the rearview mirror. "Yet."

"Good luck." Devon smiled at them in the rearview mirror. "You look really good."

Lia patted Gem's shoulder. When the group arrived at Ben's house, Gem looked in the mirror once and nodded. Devon jumped out and held the door open. Lia and Devon walked to the door a few steps behind Gem, who knocked with a shaking hand.

May opened the door. "Ben! Your murder friends are here!" she shouted up the stairs behind her. She leaned on the door with one arm stretched to the top of it, all six feet of her taking up the whole entranceway. She looked like some flirtatious knight who could kick your butt or carry it over the threshold. She tapped her fingers against the frame. "I hear you're doing well."

"Yeah," Gem said. "We've gotten two people."

"Nice," May said.

Devon leaned down and whispered in Lia's ear, "You look good, by the way."

"Thank you," Lia whispered back.

His lips brushed her ear, as if he were about to say something else.

"Yes!" Ben thundered down the stairs and skidded across the floor. He bowed over one arm and gestured deeper into the house. "After y'all."

They stepped inside. May shut and locked the door behind them. Ben and May's parents were rich in a way that made Lia's stomach hurt. The house had to have five bedrooms, and she was sure the kitchen that Ben led them through was bigger than any she'd ever seen. The five of them wandered out into the large backyard. Ben pointed to a small houselike shed against the far fence.

"I've got food, drinks, and enough games to keep us busy for three years," Ben said. "What do you want to do first?"

"He loves hosting," May whispered in Gem's ear, her hand on their shoulder. "He's like an old lady. If he could major in 'party throwing,' he would."

"Old ladies can do whatever they want," Ben said. "It's not an insult."

"I'll give you my grandmother's recipe for ambrosia salad, and then you'll be halfway to full old-lady-hood," offered Lia.

Ben clapped her on the shoulder slightly too hard. "I'll be unstoppable at potlucks."

"God help us if you figure out how to make doilies." Gem laughed. "I'm good with playing Smash and eating. What are you doing tonight?"

"I could eat," said May, eyes never leaving Gem. "And if any of you lose to Ben, I'm kicking you out."

Devon snorted. "Should I leave now, then?"

"No, I'll teach you," Lia said. "After I win a few times."

"You two can sneak off later. I'll teach you how to play," Ben said, rubbing his hands together. "Come on."

The inside of the guesthouse was one room with a kitchen-ette and attached bathroom. Lia dropped into an old beanbag, and Devon fell onto the couch behind her. May and Gem talked about the gym and other things Lia couldn't quite hear until they all started playing "Pictionary but better" as Ben put it, and Lia didn't have the heart to correct him. Devon was a terrible drawer but Lia was excellent, and he wrapped one arm around her waist, pulling her up and off the couch to keep her from beating him again. She landed half in his lap, face to his chest, and he wrapped his arms around her so that she couldn't move her hands to draw. She laughed into his shoulder.

She wasn't used to playing group games. It was nice.

Lia knocked Devon's chin with her forehead. "Free me."

This was so much better.

"Not a chance," he said. "You should have to draw with your toes. It's not fair."

His grip loosened during the next round. She leaned across his lap, her head on the arm of the couch and his arms resting on her stomach. She glanced up at him and caught his eyes on her. He looked away.

He lost that round, too.

"All right," Devon said. "I have to take a break. This is terrible for my ego. Prince is a monster."

An odd little thrill threaded its way through Lia's belly. She was good at this, and she was finally getting to show that off. Devon didn't seem to really mind losing, though. "I could use a break, too. Want to walk around?"

"Yes!" May slipped from the couch to the floor next to Gem. "Finally someone else can have a shot at winning."

Devon shrugged and helped Lia up from the beanbag. They wandered outside into the backyard, their path lit by fairy lights. Devon didn't let go of her hand, the soft tug of his fingers leading her to a lit alcove full of lavender stalks and mums. He sat on a little stone bench and Lia sat next to him. The cold crept between them. Lia scooted closer to him.

Devon curled his arm around her. "Okay?" he asked.

"No," she said, and he pulled away. "Wait. No. I just mean this would be okay if I weren't so short."

They moved from the bench to the grass. She stretched her legs out across the lawn, and nestled the back of her head in the crook of his right elbow. Her side was pressed to his warm chest. His leg shook beneath her back. Lia pulled his left arm across her waist. He laid his hand against her side.

"I like listening to you talk." Devon sighed, his fingers tapping against her hip. "You used to talk all the time in class."

"I got in trouble all the time, too." Lia swallowed. She talked too much when she got started—rambling off facts and going on tangents no one asked for. She never noticed until midway through a sentence, and then it was too late. "Do you really like listening to me?"

"When you talk about things you like? Yes." He rubbed the hem of her shirt between his fingers, knuckles grazing bare skin. "Physics was the best. You always talked in physics."

"You know there's a planet we can't see but is there," she said slowly, trying to remember something she hadn't talked about in physics. His hand, warm and soft, flattened against her skin beneath her shirt. Her breathing quickened. "We only know it's there because everything we can see reacts to it in some way. Invisible but consequential. I feel like that sometimes."

"You have an interesting take on romance." He chuckled.

Lia turned her face to look at him. "It's true. You never notice me."

"I always notice you," he said. "I hate that you sit behind me in biology. Makes me nervous. What if I do something embarrassing? You'll write it down in that little leather journal."

"That's my Assassins journal. I wouldn't write about you in it, and it's gone anyway. I left it in Ms. Christie's class. It had my email in it and everything, but no one messaged me to return it." Lia's skin was too warm, too tight, and her next words were a whisper. "It's my spiral journal where I write down all your embarrassing moments."

He laughed, and her head bounced against him. His heart pounded through his ribs, a steady beat she could barely hear.

"Is this supposed to be romantic?" she asked softly, voice muffled by his sweater.

"Yes, we're stargazing," he said, tilting his head back to stare at the stars. "I wanted to focus on my grades and not date anyone, and I don't know what I'm doing, but school's basically over and you're going away probably. I wasn't sure what to do. But I knew I wanted to get to know you."

"So you joined the game." She brought her right hand up to his face and traced a line from the corner of his mouth to his eye. "You joined the game to talk to me?"

He licked his lips. "That about sums it up."

He shifted beneath her, and Lia sat up. She cupped his face, turning him to face her. Stars filled his dark eyes.

"You know I've liked you since seventh grade, right?" she asked.

"What?" His fingers pressed into her hip. "No. Really?"

Lia nodded. She could feel the stars in him, the promise of a future and life. It was heat and tenderness, the way his hand seared without hurting, and he tilted his head to the side. The moonlight struck his skin and glittered like frost on autumn leaves. He had joined to be close to her. He had wanted to be close to her.

And she wanted to live.

Lia leaned in till her mouth was an inch from his. His lips brushed Lia's, but he didn't move closer. She laced her fingers around the back of his neck and pulled his mouth to hers. His breath caught and his fingers tightened. The kiss carried on until the thundering of their hearts became footsteps heading their way.

"So," he said, and pulled away. His hand stroked her spine through her shirt. "Strategically, we're doing great."

"Well, your plan succeeded," she said, a coil of thrill tightening in her belly. His plan had been to get closer to her! Her! He didn't want to kill her after all. Well, maybe he did, but gently. "Mine is still in the works."

"You'll win." He laced his fingers with hers and helped her up. "I believe in you."

And as much as she loved the words, they hurt. She couldn't remember the last time someone had.

CHAPTER 17

They left Ben's at 11:30, and Gem dropped Lia off at her house. Devon hadn't kissed her goodbye, not in Gem's car, but he hadn't let go of her hand until she had opened the car door. They hadn't talked much more in the alcove, but they had kissed there. A lot.

That seemed much better than talking.

The last two hours at Ben's had been spent playing games, and now, back at home, Lia's mind was racing as quickly as her heart.

She'd made out with Devon! He had said he liked her! He had joined the game to spend time with her!

Lia pressed her back to the front door, slid down it, and buried her face in her knees. His hands were as lovely as she'd always imagined. She couldn't let the game end now that they finally had something to do together.

"Lia?" her mom's voice called from the dark.

"Yes?"

"Just making sure it's you," her mom said. "How'd it go?"

"Great!" Lia said, and she was sure her voice broke. "I'm going to sleep and then Ben's picking us up in the morning for more game stuff."

Her mom sighed, still half in the dark. "Okay, get plenty of rest."

"I will."

Lia's phone vibrated, and she pulled it out. The light blinded her.

> All my assassinssssssssssssssssssssssssssssssssssssssssssssssssss home alive?

Ben had asked at midnight. It took them all a while to respond, but when they all had an hour later, he'd said:

> Good. Sleep well

Lia did.

Except she woke up half an hour after Ben was supposed to pick her up, and her phone had five messages waiting for her.

Have you heard from Ben? Gem had asked twice.

Devon had replied, No. He's late for me too

> Lia?
> You there?

Lia responded and dashed to the bathroom.

> **I'm here. Maybe he overslept? I did**

Gem said: Let me steal the car, and we can see what's up. I bet he's asleep

But an uneasy ache wound itself around Lia's chest as she got into Gem's car half an hour later. Their plan to meet up and discuss their new target—Nora from Ben's English class—and figure out how to keep Gem and Devon safe from their assassins was put on hold. Lia's assassin still hadn't made themselves known. It was oddly insulting.

The Barnard house was dark when they arrived. The sun had long come up, making empty eyes of the windows bearing down on them. Lia hung back as Devon rang the doorbell, but no one answered. Gem banged on the door for a bit before texting May. She was a few blocks over at a friend's house. Finally, the three of them hopped the tall wooden fence leading to the backyard.

The patio table was overturned. Broken glass littered the stones and crunched beneath their shoes. The chairs were sideways and broken, legs hanging on by thin strips of wood. Blood, dark and dry, stained the outside wall in a splattered arc. Gem screamed.

"Ben!" Lia darted forward. Last time, she had been dazed. Last time, she had done nothing. "No, no, no, no."

She leapt over a fallen chair and stumbled to her knees. Ben, unmoving, lay facedown on the patio. The broken glass bit into her knees, and Ben didn't move or moan when she turned him over. Cuts and scratches peppered the bare skin of his arms. Lia shoved her shoulder against his. He fell onto his back. His head lolled to the side.

The skin around his mouth and nose was red and bubbled as if he had been badly burned. A small silver knife was lodged deep into his left eye. Long gashes had torn his shirt to shreds, and his hand slipped off his chest. The fingers were bent back, bones snapped clean through the skin. The skin from fingertips to elbow was red, raw, and blistered. Lia gagged.

Devon's voice rumbled behind her, thick and slurred. Gem's hands closed around her shoulders and pulled her back. Their voice, too, spluttered and slowed, and Lia tried to tell them they weren't making any sense, she couldn't hear her own voice. A high-pitched whine built in her ears. Her eyes burned.

Lia vomited against the fence, far away from Ben, and wiped her mouth.

"I don't know how long. . . . No, he's not, I mean, there's no way. . . . No, it's just us. . . . The backyard," Devon said into his phone. His free hand was over his eyes, and his head was tilted back. Tears dripped down either side of his face. "Please hurry."

"What did they do to him?" Gem cried.

Lia closed her eyes and shook her head. "His hand. His fingers. They broke his fingers."

"He's in the same clothes," Devon said. His voice cracked, and he didn't move from his spot in the yard, only a few steps from Ben's body. Still, he didn't look down. "He's in the same clothes from last night, but he messaged us. He messaged us."

"May can't be here. She can't," Gem whispered.

Gem fled the backyard. Lia chased after, gripping Gem's hand when they heaved into the bushes. Devon joined them, still on the phone with 911. The voice at the other end rambled on. Lia shuddered.

"Do you know what time you left last night?" the person on the other end was asking.

Devon opened his mouth, blinked, and lost the words. He stared at Lia, shaking his head as the 911 operator repeated the question, and Lia reached out to hit the speaker button. He closed his eyes.

"I think we left before midnight," Lia said. "And he's in the same clothes as then."

Devon leaned his forehead against Lia's, and they each mumbled answers to the operator whenever the other couldn't find the strength to answer. Soon, blue and red lights flickered down the street. The world slowed and blurred again like it had with Abby, but this time it was so much worse.

The paramedics showed up first. They checked over Gem, Devon, and Lia before stepping aside. The cops, the same ones Lia had met barely two weeks ago, questioned them and catalogued their shoes and fingerprints. One swabbed the blood soaking Lia's pants and called the paramedics back over. The glass had cut her knees. Their parents were called, and Lia could hear the confusion in her mom's voice.

"You turn him over?" one of the detectives; Lia recognized him but couldn't remember his name.

The paramedic shook her head. "DOA. They did."

He glanced over at them. Lia ducked her head, desperate to be smaller. The detective took a step toward them, and a shriek rang out across the street.

May.

The paramedics grabbed her and calmed her down as much as they could. She sobbed against one of them. Gem and Lia held on to each other.

●　●

Lia said nothing until she was home, the door was shut and locked, and she had showered Ben's blood off of her. She could still hear May crying in her head.

"I've made an appointment with Dr. Woods for you Monday," her mom said. She sat on the edge of Lia's bed, face drawn and pale. "No arguing."

"Thank you," Lia said. She wanted to go. She wanted to talk to someone. Abby was still so fresh that she felt like a secret Lia should keep when people asked her about it, and she was sure Ben would feel the same way. "Mom, I—"

"And no more of this game," her mom interrupted her. "I know you have no control over these things, but this is too much. Twice now this stupid game has put you in danger. You're out."

"No!" Lia lurched. "Mom, the game isn't—"

"My God, Lia, what if you had still been there?" her mom asked. "What if you trip while chasing someone? What if they mistake you for a mugger? You have other things you need to think about, like your life."

If she had still been there, maybe Ben wouldn't have died.

CHAPTER 18

Lia's parents were in agreement: She wasn't allowed to play the game any longer. They didn't give her a choice, and they didn't ask for her opinion.

But Lia had done what they told her to for far too long. They talked about how dangerous it was to stay out late, to walk home alone, to talk to strangers. But Ben had been at home. Lia could think of nothing that would keep her safe from whoever killed Ben. The killer had incapacitated him with latex before even trying to kill him. The allergic reaction was all over the news.

The killer *knew* him.

"We talked to Devon's and Gem's parents," her father said on the way home from the therapist's office. He drove slower than he spoke, his fingers clenched around the wheel. "You're excused for three days. Try to focus on school and getting healthy."

Like she wasn't right now?

Her mom cleared her throat. "What your dad means is, focus on yourself. Don't feel like you have to push yourself to do anything you don't want to do."

It was high school. Students always had to push themselves.

"I want to keep playing Assassins," Lia said. "I've been looking forward to it all year and planning for it, and we're raising money for Abby."

"No," said her mom. "Absolutely not. Focus on yourself."

"And school," her father said.

If she let them know she didn't feel up to school, they'd just let her skip. Sure. Yeah. That was how that would work.

He didn't mention the deaths again after that, as if maneuvering around them would keep the grief at bay. Her mom, at least, gathered her up in a hug and settled her on the couch with a blanket. They gathered in the living room, glued to the news and their phones, and her mom repeated every hour or so about what a tragedy it was. She didn't have access to the gossip-filled chats Lia did; not everyone thought it was a tragedy.

"What an idiot," one anonymous comment read. "What sort of linebacker loses a fight?"

"The dude better be huge when they catch him."

Ben Barnard was murdered and still people found a way to twist it for laughs. The last murder in Lincoln had been five years ago, and it had been a family feud. Now there were two dead kids and dozens of rumors: Abby's death wasn't an accident. Ben had killed Abby and this was revenge. Assassins was cursed. Lia was cursed.

She stopped reading after that.

She had spoken to the police for an hour the day after Ben's death, making sure her timeline lined up with everyone else's. She couldn't even blame them.

"Maybe I am cursed," she muttered while watching the evening news with her mom.

Three days Ben had been dead, and Lia couldn't wrap her

mind around anything. There was nothing for her to do except sleep and speculate. Her teachers hadn't sent her homework— Gem and Devon said they hadn't gotten anything either—and without the game to plan for, she had nothing to fill her head. So Abby and Ben did instead.

"Lia," her mom said with that sigh of an adult holding back. "There's no such thing as curses."

"Still." Lia fiddled with her school agenda, flipping to the back pages. "Abby was my target. Ben was my teammate."

Abby Ascher—II

Ben Barnard—I

She would get a kill in his name if it killed her.

"Why on earth would a curse or a killer center their life around you?" her mom asked. "Correlation doesn't equal causation."

That didn't totally apply, but Lia let her mom have it. "Devon's calling," Lia lied. "I'm going to go talk to him."

Can we talk? Lia texted him when she got to her room. She lay back on her bed, her open agenda in one hand and her phone in the other. She ran a thumb across Abby's and Ben's names, and the pencil smeared. Lia tossed the agenda aside. About anything?

Devon's response buzzed in her palm. "Of course," he said, his voice quiet and low.

"How are you holding up?" she asked, glad that he had called and not texted.

It felt weird to ask, but Lia wasn't sure talking about anything else was appropriate. No one ever prepped teens for deaths. She'd no clue what to do or say.

"I'm okay I think," Devon said. "Did they ask you if Ben had any enemies?"

"Yeah. I told them he was the least likely person to have

enemies." Lia rolled onto her stomach and tried to separate her memories of Devon's voice and how much she loved it from how Ben's hand flopped against his dead chest with a hollow *smack*. "They kept asking about time, too."

Devon didn't say anything for several seconds. "I think he died right after we left."

Lia didn't ask why. It was Devon. He loved the weird, gross parts of biology few others did, and if he thought something, he was probably right. He deferred to her on the game; she trusted him with this.

"They wanted to hurt him. He would have died even if they hadn't stabbed him like that," Devon said. "His arms and face were broken out from an allergic reaction, and I bet he couldn't breathe. Even if he had won the fight, he wouldn't have lived."

"But how did they know about his allergy?" Lia asked.

Ben had barely wanted to tell them. She could think of no one who knew.

"I don't know," he said. "Are you going to the funeral?"

"No." Lia swallowed, throat hot and sore. "Apparently, I don't do great at them."

"Ben would probably want a party instead anyway."

He would rather be alive, but Lia couldn't even say that aloud.

"Sorry. I need to go," he said. "Text me whenever you want. I'm helping my dad cook now, but I'm not going to school for a few days."

"Okay. You too. You can message me whenever you want."

"Mom?" Lia wandered back into the living room and collapsed onto the couch next to her mom. Her dad couldn't take off work, and she wasn't sure she was upset about it. "Is it bad if I don't go to the funeral?"

"No," her mom said. "Honey, you didn't even make it through Abby's. It is perfectly fine not to go to Ben's."

Lia nodded. "I just feel bad not going, and I know it'll be closed casket, but I know what he looks like and I can't—"

"Lia, it's fine." Her mom scrolled through another news article about it. "Lord rest his soul, but I doubt Ben would have noticed you weren't there."

Lia winced. "That's not nice. He would have. He might've been goofy, but he was great."

"Lia." She put down her phone and faced her daughter. "I'm sorry. You're right, and that wasn't what I meant. Ben Barnard was a very good boy, and he certainly wouldn't want you to be sad on his account."

Lia peeked at her mom's phone: PROMISING FOOTBALL STAR STRUCK DOWN IN PRIME—RANDOM OR REVENGE?

Lia shook her head. Abby had been reduced to her promising test scores, and Ben now to his promising sport.

"Are you sadder about Abby dying?" Lia asked softly.

"I'm sad two very promising kids are gone," her mom said. "I'm sad for them and what they could be, and for their parents."

But what if Abby and Ben hadn't been promising?

"Let us look at the one bright thing that may come from this." Her mom picked up her phone again and wrapped her other arm over Lia's shoulders. "Someone else might get Abby's scholarship now and go on to do great things they might not have had a chance to do otherwise. Abby would like that."

Abby would like living, and it would suck to wonder forever if you only got a reward because someone else died.

"They haven't caught Ben's killer yet," Lia said. "They're still out there."

"Wherever he is, I am sure the police are closing in on him," her mom said. She looked up, her gaze going from Lia's face to her clenched hands. "Those families have been through enough. You're not a detective. They don't need someone stalking them and playing hero."

But she already had stalked them. She knew nearly everything about Ben's daily schedule and the daily lives of most of her classmates. Abby's death was an accident, but Ben's was intentional. How did they even know about his allergy? she wondered again.

Her phone dinged, and Lia jumped. It was the Council.

"I have homework," Lia said too quickly and too loudly. "I'm going to go do it."

She dashed to her room before her mom could respond.

Hello, assassins.

The game is not canceled. The game is never canceled. All memorials, funerals, and graveyards are now off-limits. The money collected will be split between the animal shelter and the Boys & Girls Club. Ben Barnard was one of us. But we are not of Lincoln High. It has no authority over us. Lincoln has no authority over us. The game continues no matter who tries to stop it. For every assassin who keeps playing, the Council will donate $5. For every assassin taken out, the Council will match the players' donations.

Play for Abby and Ben. Win for them.

Happy hunting,

The Council

CHAPTER 19

By Wednesday, when Lia returned to school with Gem and Devon, the halls were still filled with whispers and rumors about Ben. Lincoln was a small town, and everybody knew somebody in the know. Lia barely listened to their history teacher talking about grief counseling. She had finished her missing work the night before, and it only took a quarter of class to finish the new homework due Friday. Instead of taking notes, she went over her list of possible Assassins players.

If she didn't, if she stopped thinking about school or the game, she would think about Abby and Ben. She couldn't think about them yet.

Much of the class couldn't seem to either. No one was in their regular seat, not even Faith. She had swapped with Georgia so that Abby's best friend didn't have to sit near an empty chair.

"And finally," said Ms. Christie, straightening the papers in her hands, "I believe you'll all be getting emails today detailing how that little game you all play every year is banned on school grounds. Anyone still found playing after today will be given in-school suspension for three days minimum, and repeat offenders will not be allowed to walk at graduation. This is, of course, for your safety."

Lia's fingers clenched around her pen. "What?"

Faith glanced sideways at Lia, and Devon touched her shoulder from his seat behind her.

"Assassins," Ms. Christie said, looking at Lia. "No more of that unless you want in-school suspension."

Lia didn't listen to anything after that.

A few hours later, outside at lunch, Devon sat next to her and held up his hand before she could talk. "I'm thinking about withdrawing from the game. I don't really want to talk about it, but I wanted to let you know."

An uneasy energy settled in Lia, and she tapped her heels against the ground. This was the first time they had ever gotten to spend time together, and now it was almost over.

"I'm not getting in-school suspension or banned from walking," Devon went on, trying to convince Lia as well as himself. "My mom doesn't want me walking around outside anymore either."

"You don't have to go out," Lia said. "Please. We can keep playing from inside the safety of Gem's car."

"I haven't decided," he said. "I was only putting it on the table."

"Ben was home," Lia whispered. "They were in his backyard, and they stabbed him so hard they couldn't get the knife out. They wore latex gloves so he couldn't fight back. Not playing isn't going to keep us safe. If anything, we should spend more time together."

"But it might keep us safer, especially since they don't know who killed Ben." Devon unsnapped his lunch box and pulled out a sandwich. "Or why."

"Yeah, but what's the likelihood it's a serial killer?" Lia asked, picking at the knot of the Kroger bag she used for lunch. "Isn't it always a family member or friend? We could win, and if we donate a lot, they have to match it."

Devon waved to someone behind Lia and shook his head. "We can donate and volunteer without wandering around in the dark."

"It's not like we would be alone like Ben," mumbled Lia. They shouldn't have left. They should've stayed. They should've done anything else. "Our grief is making serial killers out of circumstance."

"Pithy but too late," Devon said. "Faith, you still want to swap?"

The other girl appeared near Lia's left shoulder and sat delicately at the end of the plastic bench. She pulled a paper napkin out of her metal lunch box and laid it on her knee. Devon handed her a sandwich bag of crackers. She set a knob of tinfoil in front of him.

"Wow," Gem said. "This is the most secretive I've ever seen you. A lunchtime swap, mysterious tinfoil. It's so clandestine."

Faith laughed. "I don't like eating garlic bread at school."

"Fair." Lia took a sip of her water to hide her wince. She hadn't heard such a loud laugh since before Ben. "You can stay and eat with us."

"Thanks, but I do not do the cold." She wiggled her gloved fingers as if playing a piano and tossed her fancy silverware, new crackers, and napkin back into her lunch bag. "My fingers get all shaky, and I told Georgia I'd eat with her."

She waved goodbye, and Lia ripped the handles off her lunch bag. A team of two people was at a severe disadvantage, but Lia had been planning for months. Maybe she could do it alone.

"I'm going to keep playing," Lia told him. "I hope you do, too."

Devon got up abruptly. "I'll let you know." And then he walked away.

"So I guess you're not dating, then?" Gem asked.

Lia groaned. "I don't know. I just don't want to think and can't think and need to think about something not Abby or Ben, and Assassins is that for me right now." She picked up Devon's forgotten garlic bread, peeled back the foil, and tossed a piece into the bushes. A robin pecked at the bread and dragged a chunk back to a small tree.

"You want to get milkshakes and see if we can knock Nora out after school?" Gem asked.

Lia nodded.

The rest of the day was a blur. Lia didn't have another class with Devon, and though they had texted over the last few days, they hadn't talked about what happened at Ben's party. Death put a damper on dating.

I just feel weird about it is all, he texted her, unprompted, during third period. It's a game, and you're treating it like it's real.

She had no idea how to respond to that, so she settled on Okay.

It was bad.

"So," Gem said as they sat in their car after school. "Nora."

"She goes to that big park down by the river after school before heading home," Lia said. "Jogs, does resistance training, and yoga, depending on the day."

"Okay." Gem started the car. "Let's go fake-kill Nora."

They grabbed milkshakes and snacks, and Gem pulled over outside the park. It was one of those private parks owned by a homeowners association, and the gate to get into the lot was locked, a lone woman enjoying the solitude of the park and snapping selfies in front of the flower beds. They would have to get Nora on her way in or out, or find a way inside. Gem cracked a window and Lia pushed her seatback down.

"So you and Devon vanished for a while the other night." Gem sipped their drink. "Have fun?"

Lia sank down in her seat. "Yes."

"You want to expand on that?"

"Not really," Lia said. "I feel sort of guilty about it now. You know."

Gem sucked on their teeth and nodded. "I don't know if I should message May condolences or something. It feels . . ."

"Like we left him to die but not really?" Lia offered.

"Yeah," Gem said. "What if we'd stayed later? What if we'd gotten there earlier?"

"What ifs don't bring people back. They just make us worry," Lia whispered. Her therapist had told her that. "They might have just killed him the next time he was alone. We were just orbiting."

If death were a planet, Abby's and Ben's families were rings. Lia and Gem were distant moons or cold, observant stars.

"If we keep this conversation up, I will cry, so I'm throwing you under the bus," Gem said. "You and Devon make out?"

"Oh my God." Lia folded over her knees but nodded. "What does it mean?"

Gem practically squealed. "It means you were wrong all these years!"

"But it's not good circumstances," Lia said. "At all."

"Are you still talking?"

"Yeah," Lia said, "and I'll see him tomorrow in class."

"Amazing," Gem said.

"Are you just excited because I was wrong?" Lia asked.

"Blah blah blah I'm happy for you whatever." Gem waved their hand. "So rarely can I say 'I told you so.' Let me have this."

"What do I even say to him?" Lia groaned. "Hey, I know our friend died after we made out, but are we official or is it a casual thing?"

"Add a heart emoji to the end, but yeah." Gem leaned forward and touched Lia's arm. "Nora's here. She didn't withdraw, so this is fine, right?"

"I guess?"

Lia peeked over the edge of the door. Nora—a short girl sporting a swimsuit under her T-shirt and a scarf knotted protectively over her hair—walked a small collie and read something on her phone. A water gun was tucked into the pocket of her joggers.

"What do your notes say about Nora?" Gem asked, pulling a water gun out of the backseat.

Lia laughed softly. "Smart, prepared, probably can't be caught unawares."

"Cool," Gem said. "Can you see her?"

Lia rifled through her bag and came up empty. "I can't find my binoculars," she said. "Maybe my mom took them back."

She hadn't wanted to loan them to Lia in the first place, and now she had probably taken them back as a way to make sure Lia stopped playing.

"Sounds like something she'd do," Gem said. "That other lady is leaving, but unless you're a better shot than that first attempt, we won't be able to hit Nora from beyond the fence. People will probably show up before she leaves."

"There's a play group that comes by in twenty minutes. We'll be overrun by toddlers," Lia said. "Could we have one thing go right?"

Gem exhaled loudly. "This would be so much easier if Lincoln had fewer dog lovers. I have an idea, but it's going to get us disqualified if I'm caught."

Nora vanished over the little hill to the dog park. Gem got out of the car, armed with only a phone. Lia watched as Gem slunk to the entrance to the lot, out of sight of the woman leaving, and started walking along the sidewalk toward the gate as if simply out for a stroll. Gem stared at the phone in their hand. The woman who was leaving shut the gate behind her and dropped her key into her pocket. She too stared at her phone.

Gem ran into her, apologizing and fluttering about, one hand on the woman's arm and the other patting her down to make sure she was okay. It was a classic distraction, one Gem used often when showing off simple tricks. Gem and the woman laughed and chatted. Then, they went their separate ways. As Gem walked toward the gate, they flashed their palm to Lia. Silver glinted in it.

Just the one key, Gem texted. Thank God. I'd feel weird stealing all her keys.

You're amazing. Lia, laughing, got out of the car and close enough to the park to watch.

Gem kept their head down and both hands on their phone. With no sudden movements, Nora didn't look up, and Gem got within range without even the dog noticing. Gem lingered near a bench, and Nora set her phone aside. Gem lifted their water gun and fired. Water splashed against Nora's back.

Lia whooped. They all joined up and exchanged details and plans. Nora was a good sport and a touch relieved—she had grown tired of being on edge. Nora left to change, and Gem and Lia chased down the woman to return her "dropped" key. As they returned to Gem's car, Gem wrapped one arm around Lia.

"I know we're probably not going to the same school after this and I'm technically leaving," Gem said, "but I'm not leaving *you*."

"I know," Lia whispered.

"Do you?" Gem asked. "Because you're being weird about this."

"I just . . ." Lia leaned her cheek against Gem's shoulder. "Everything is about to change, and I know you haven't decided yet, but wherever it is, I'm not going. And that's fine, but we've not been apart since third grade. It's weird. I don't like it." Lia rolled her eyes. "I mean, I like you going to college. That's great. I don't like not knowing when we'll next spend time together. This is it, and this was it on spending time with Devon."

Gem's eyes narrowed. "I have *another* idea."

CHAPTER 20

Devon's parents, though skeptical, agreed to let Devon spend the night at Gem's with Lia so long as all of them were in the living room and their hands were in sight at all times. Gem assumed Devon was joking about that. Lia wasn't so sure.

"What?" Gem asked as they sat in the car and finished off the last of their snacks. "Like you're going to go at it while I'm right there?"

Gem fake heaved, and Lia forced herself to smile. She knew she should have laughed. If it were any other day, she would have, but it was today and she felt like happiness was a dream. Maybe if she faked it, she would be happy. There'd been a moment with Gem after Nora was out that she felt vaguely happy. It had faded as fast as it had come, though.

"Ask your mom," Gem said. "I want to get home."

Lia's mom was easier to convince; Lia had spent enough time at Gem's over the last decade, but Devon's presence was just a new wrinkle between her mom's brows. Gem's mom worked in security and promised to keep an eye on the three. Ben's killer was still on the loose anyway. Gem's house was safer.

They agreed to it, Devon texted them midway through their parents' three-way phone call. Now they're just talking about Ben.

Lia pushed open the car door. "Let's clean up before we head back, then."

The last few days of driving everyone around had tracked in dead leaves and mud. Gem tossed several empty cans to Lia and pulled the floor mats out of their car. Lia bent over the back of the car and gathered up every piece of junk she could find. Arms full, she stood and looked for the trash can. It was bolted to a post at the edge of the parking lot. Behind it stood a hooded figure.

Lia froze, but the figure didn't. They were short and hooded, and their hands were tucked into their pockets. Lia couldn't make out their face. Gem shook out another floor mat.

"Lia, just toss it." Gem looked up at her. "What are you doing?"

"Turn around," Lia said.

Gem's eyes widened, and they pivoted. The figure in the distance waved. That was far too friendly for a murderer. Probably.

"Well, screw that," Gem said. "Let's get out of here."

By the time they had locked the car doors, the figure was gone. They had vanished over the crest of the hill and into the neighborhood around the park. Gem kept their water gun up and ready to go. Lia raced to the trash can to toss their trash and studied the footprints near it.

Converse. Not helpful.

"It's my assassin, right?" Lia asked. "Not—"

"Yeah, has to be. They waved." Gem laughed. "We're fine. We're paranoid, but we're fine."

"Let's just go." Lia walked backward to the car, one hand clasped tightly around Gem's jacket. There was no movement in the trees. As they drove away, light flickered twice in the distance like two glowing eyes, but they turned a corner and it was gone.

Lia sank down into her seat. "Of course they pick now to show their face."

"Who do you think it is?" Gem asked.

They spent the whole car ride and the hour after at Gem's house discussing it, but they were no closer to a definite answer when Devon showed up.

He fiddled with the straps of his bag and lingered in the entryway. "I'm glad you guys invited me. I keep having weird dreams and stuff. You know."

"Yeah," Gem said, "we know."

They all knew what Ben looked like dead, and there was no one else they could talk to about that.

"Come on." Gem clapped him on the shoulder and nodded toward the living room. "I think we all need this."

The Hastings' house was an odd mix of old, sagging furniture covered in blankets, half-put-together computers, and crafting supplies. Otter, the family cat, wove her way between their legs and beneath the coffee table to sniff at Devon until she was satisfied.

Mr. Hastings came back inside, and Otter scrambled up his legs until he gathered her up like a baby.

"Now, we're supposed to keep an eye on you, which should be easy," Mr. Hastings said. He locked the door behind himself, and the security system let out a comforting beep. "Lia, we haven't seen you outside of school since eighth grade. We have a lot of catching up to do."

Mr. Hastings put them through all the usual questions and recruited them to help cook dinner. Devon chopped onions while

Gem minced garlic, and Lia, in charge of making the rice, dabbed at Devon's stinging eyes with a dishcloth when the onions became too much. Mr. Hastings kept an eye on them as he dealt with the chicken. Mrs. Hastings got home with Gem's brother just as dinner was ready.

Over dinner, they talked about school and orchestra, the game a little bit, and Gem's disastrous attempts at carpentry for the school play, and everything except the deaths. Gem's little brother Harrison was in band and talked to Devon about music nonstop. No one else in the family played, and Devon didn't seem to mind. Mrs. Hastings only stopped Harrison when he forgot to eat.

It was a sort of love Lia couldn't comprehend. Gem's parents didn't care what their kids wanted to do but went all in every time. Lia's parents had tried to curate her high school years as if she were an art gallery only open to college admissions.

"I told them to cool it on questions about how you are," Gem whispered after their mom had asked about how Lia was liking school. "Sorry. I don't know how long it will last."

Lia laughed and smiled. "With any luck, they'll be too into talking about orchestra with Devon."

Her mom kept texting about the "sleepover" and what they would do after, and it made Lia feel like a toddler. That was probably on purpose.

But more than anything, it felt like a normal, happy night.

● ●

The house creaked all night long after everyone crawled into bed. It had been easy to forget the horrors outside while everyone was awake, Devon helping Harrison with his music homework and

Lia destroying Mr. Hastings in a game of Risk in record time. There was no pressure. There was no threat.

It was harder to not see Abby and Ben every time Lia closed her eyes once the main light went out and the dark oozed around her.

"I keep thinking about Omelet," whispered Lia. "He didn't want to leave Abby."

"I'm glad we found Ben." Gem reached underneath the blankets and laced their fingers with Lia's. "If we hadn't, May would have."

Gem's parents had left their bedroom door open, and Devon had been banished to a sleeping bag on the far side of the room. Of course, once everyone else had left, he had dragged it nearer to Lia so that they could talk.

Lia shuddered. His sleeping bag rustled. Fingers gently touched the ends of her hair.

"You need more sleep," he said softly, as if she were an easily spooked cat.

"We all do." She licked her lips and turned to face him. "Have you been sleeping?"

"You know I haven't been," he replied. "It's weird that it happened so soon after Abby."

"They questioned me longer after Ben," Lia said. Two kids in Lincoln, both playing the game, dead within two weeks of each other. "What could Ben have ever done that someone would want to kill him?"

Whoever had been after Ben had enjoyed killing him, and that made it so much worse.

"Maybe they just wanted to kill somebody," Gem said. "Some people like killing."

Lia shuddered. "I think the police thought I did it, a little bit, at first."

"I'm pretty sure Omelet would have eaten you if you hurt Abby." Devon's long fingers wove their way through her hair, curling the ends. In the dark, she could only see the soft glint of his eyes. "Abby tripped, and what reason would you even have for killing Ben?"

"His assassin got him? I don't know." She shook her head and sighed. "I keep thinking about his hand. That was where he got shot, and they destroyed it."

"I know we're here to talk," Gem said, "but I don't know if I can handle this level of gruesome before sleeping."

"Sorry," Lia said. "Have your parents been doing that thing where they only mention how sad it is that their plans were cut short?"

Devon groaned. "No, but my mom's friend did. Such bright futures snuffed out too soon."

"Just as bad." Lia brought one hand up to Devon's face. "I hate it."

Her fingertips brushed his jaw. She had never imagined sleeping near him. That seemed intimate and tender, like sharing a cup of tea or a deep, dark secret. She traced the slant of his jaw and the arch of his nose, felt the slight bump of a scar near his ear and the flutter of his lashes against her knuckles, and she rested her hand against his cheek. He ran his hand from her scalp to her shoulders.

"Having plans doesn't make a person more valuable," Devon whispered. He booped her nose.

"If I hear one more person lament the loss of Abby but not Ben because of how promising she was, I'll scream. They always bring up his football as if they need to find something for him to be good at for him to be worth mourning." Gem, on their back and glaring at the ceiling, rolled their head back and forth. "It's so . . ."

"Gross?" Lia offered.

Devon snorted. "That's one word for it, and not the one I would use."

"Do you think the school would be as sad if it were other kids?" Lia turned over onto her stomach. "Not the other students but like the teachers? Principal White?"

"They would say yes," Gem said, "but they're liars. They make such a big deal out of college and life plans."

Lia folded one arm under her cheek and lay the other near Devon's shoulder. Cheek squished against her arm, sight slightly blurred, she closed her eyes. There was no danger here.

"I have no clue what I'm doing," Lia said. "I wonder what they would say if it had been me."

Even the idea was selfish in her mouth, drying out the words till her tongue stuck to her teeth.

"Remember Mr. Allen?" Gem asked. "He told me not to bother with law school. He said I would be better suited to a liberal arts degree."

Devon gagged. "What does he think people study before law school?"

"Who knows?" Gem said. "And who cares? People work! People exist! Some don't even do high school! They're the ones up in arms over shoving us into majors."

"Devon, how did you know you wanted to be a doctor?" Lia asked.

Devon shifted onto his back, his silhouette like the sharp peaks of a cliff against the dim light filtering in from outside. "I broke my arm the summer of seventh grade and the doctor was really nice. She worked in the ER, and my mom is a doctor, but dermatology was never really interesting. I could sort of see myself being there one day? I might change my mind. I think a lot of people do."

"My cousin didn't realize until her first gross lab that she couldn't do corpses." Gem hugged Lia and pulled away. "She does research now."

"Yeah, we'll find out if I vomit, I guess," he said, and swallowed.

They all knew he wouldn't. He hadn't when they had found Ben.

"I didn't know what to do before all this happened." Lia reached out and traced the crests and dips of Devon's face. His breath warmed her skin. "Now what?"

"You don't have to go to college right out of high school, you know," Gem said. "You could work for a while or do trade school. They just don't like telling us those options."

They weren't prestigious enough. That was the implication. But Lia was already the less-than-ideal student. To be average was to be invisible.

"I know," Lia said, "but I still feel like a failure sometimes."

It was impossible not to. They started studying for the ACT and SAT in middle school, and even before that they had to pass the state tests. Schools took out newspaper ads—as if it were 1970—to advertise their students' college choices with no options for kids who were taking a break, working, or going to trade school. Most of the counselors at Lincoln were nice and kept community college information on hand, but the principal never even mentioned it when talking about futures during school assemblies. It was as clear as day in the ways Abby's death was cast against Ben's. If he weren't a football star, people might have written his loss off altogether.

It made Lia sick.

Gem yawned and rolled over. "I'm going to put my earbuds in. Don't be weird and make me regret this."

Lia glanced at Devon. "Do people think we're incapable of being alone together?"

"Yeah, I think so." He pushed himself up onto his elbows and dropped his chin onto his hands. "You're really good at puzzles."

"Thank you?" Lia exhaled. "Not like that will get me far in life. The escape room has already been invented."

"Who would want to leave a room you're in anyway?" he asked.

Lia leaned forward and pressed her lips to his, and suddenly his hand was tangled in her hair. His gasp died against her lips, and he tilted his head till their noses were pressed together. His thumb stroked her ear. Lia pulled away. He kissed the tip of her nose.

"I would rather not betray the trust of the people who are basically my second set of parents," Lia said, "but you're not going back to the other side of the room, right?"

CHAPTER 21

Lia woke slowly, light searing a white line across her eyelids. Gem snored softly to her left, a comforting sound she would know anywhere, and Otter's collar jingled as she picked her way across Lia's legs. Lia rolled over and opened her eyes to a sleeping Devon. It was early, maybe five minutes before their alarms would go off, and the only light was a thin strip escaping from underneath the bathroom door. She laid her head against his side, the steady hum of life in his veins overpowering the distant thump of his heart. His fingers brushed her neck.

"I would never have thought Gem snored," he whispered.

The bathroom door creaked, and Lia shot up. Devon chuckled.

Gem groaned and rolled over. "Time?"

"Time." Lia yawned. "Are you going to school today?"

"Emotionally, no. Physically, yes," Devon said. He rifled through his bag. "I have orchestra rehearsal after, too."

"Relatable." Lia sighed. "I can't believe we were allowed to sleep in the same room."

Lia wasn't entirely sure her parents knew about her eternal crush on Devon, but Devon's knew. God, why?

"I have used up all my sleepover goodwill, I think." Devon pushed a pair of glasses onto his face and blinked, grinning. "Good morning!"

Lia flushed. Yesterday was so hectic that Lia hadn't thought about how her normal pajamas were a T-shirt and shorts, neither particularly nice. And now he was staring at her.

"You look nice in your glasses," she said, desperate for a distraction. She gently tapped the clear plastic bridge of his glasses. "They're cute."

He rolled his eyes. "They make me look twelve."

"Yeah, but like a distinguished twelve," Gem said. They scrolled through their notifications. "Like anime protagonist twelve, the sort who somehow runs a demon-hunting business or something."

"A twelve-year-old who knows how to file taxes," Lia said.

"I'm going to put on my contacts," he muttered. "Never again."

"Wait." Gem thrust their phone beneath Lia and Devon's faces. "Look."

A handful of people online were talking about the police reopening Abby's case now that all the lab work was back. There was only speculation, no evidence. All they had said was that they weren't comfortable closing it as an accidental death yet.

"I was there," Lia said. "I heard her trip. I tripped. I had a bruise to prove it."

"They're keeping their minds open so as not to miss anything, it says." Devon handed Gem back their phone. "Ignore it. Thinking about it will just worry us."

"Sure." Lia sighed, rubbed her face, and undid the short braid of brown hanging over her shoulder. "We definitely shouldn't worry more."

They got ready in silence, trying not to wake up Harrison. When they were ready, Gem drove, and Lia sat in the passenger seat. She scratched her arms.

"You're definitely worrying," Gem said as they pulled into the parking lot.

Lia tugged her sleeves down over her hands. "If someone killed Abby, why didn't they kill me?"

Gem and Devon glanced at each other.

"There's no use in obsessing over it." Devon slipped his hand between the door and Lia's seat. His fingers gently curled around her arm. "Same rules as playing Assassins. Don't go anywhere alone and stay on guard."

"My assassin made themselves known yesterday." Lia let her head hit the back of her seat. "I hope that was my assassin."

"It was," Gem said, "and they were just angry you caught them trying to be edgy."

Lia laughed, the sound an odd bubbling thing that she didn't recognize, and followed Gem and Devon into school. The rest of the day went like that laugh—odd and fleeting. The teachers taught like normal, ignoring the empty seats and reading the announcement about grief counselors as if it were any other announcement. So quickly had the school buckled down and gotten over its grief.

She escaped to the little outdoor path from the school to the library for fresh air between her first two classes. Eyes closed, Lia tilted her head up, inhaled, and choked. The sweet, sour scent of death rolled down the back of her throat. Lia shook her head and rubbed her eyes. A robin lay rotting in the bushes near her and Gem's usual lunch table. She darted across the path.

A body smacked into her.

"Hey!" A hand closed around Lia's arm. "Oh."

It was Faith, and she dropped Lia's arm. Lia stumbled back. Her backpack fell off her shoulder.

"Crap." Faith held up her hands in surrender. "Sorry. I was just trying to slip past you. You looked pretty out of it."

Lia's stomach was in her throat. "Sorry. Yeah. I just needed fresh air."

"Good luck," Faith said with a laugh, and nodded to the bird. "Here. Let me help."

Faith set down the stack of books she had been carrying. She bent over Lia's backpack and picked it up, shoving a few of Lia's books and pens back into the half-closed front pocket. She zipped it up and handed it to Lia. Her arm didn't even shake.

Carrying textbooks was practically weight training now.

"Thanks," Lia said. "You didn't have to. It was my fault."

Faith's head cocked to the side, her hair tumbling over her shoulder. She smiled. "I feel guilty, and Mrs. White always lectures us about how important volunteering is. Consider this altruism."

"Luckily we're done with all that," Lia said, turning around and relenting.

"Hardly. I haven't heard back yet," said Faith. "But I have a four point two, so it should be fine."

Lia didn't really know how to respond to that without starting a conversation, so she only nodded.

"It would've been better, but AP World History was so pointless." She picked up her books. "Did you take it? We'll never need it."

Lia hadn't, but she had liked the last geography and civics classes she took. AP classes were the bane of her existence, and she only took the ones her parents made her take.

"You will," Lia said. "Critical reasoning and all that. You might not ever need to know when things happened, but it's the thinking that counts."

"No," said Faith, checking her phone, "I'm pretty sure you mean 'it's the thought that counts.'"

Lia did not mean that.

"Sure," Lia said. "You're right."

Faith grinned. "Sorry about spooking you. See you in class tomorrow, I guess."

"Yeah, tomorrow," Lia said, racing away. She was half worried about being late and half desperate to escape. She walked through the door to her next class with a minute to spare.

Gem was already in their seat and chatting with a beaming Cassidy.

"At least something good is happening," Gem said, smiling at her.

"What's up?" Lia asked.

"Nothing," said Cassidy quickly. Her smile fell. "I got some good news."

Lia sat without arguing. Cassidy's business was her own, but Gem leaned against their desk.

"She won't mind," Gem said. "Really?"

Lia winced. "Why would I mind good news?"

It made her feel bad; she didn't want her mere presence to take away from people's joy.

"I got offered the Governor's Scholarship," Cassidy said slowly, and she touched the little black and orange college pin on her shirt. "I was next in line for it apparently."

Because Abby was dead, the scholarship and the full ride that went with it were Cassidy's now.

"That's great!" Lia sank into her chair. Bad things had happened, and here was the proof that hope lived. "I'm really glad you got it."

• ●

The joy lasted until the end of school when Lia caught sight of Devon heading for her and Gem. Her shoulders tensed.

"Breathe," whispered Gem. "Most people prefer people who breathe."

"I hate you." Lia managed to wave back at Devon. What even were they now? He told her he'd told his parents about her. He'd slept next to her. "Hey."

"Hey," he said. "How are you?"

"I've been better," Lia said. "How are you?"

He raised and lowered one shoulder. "You know. There were good parts to today, but most of those were before school started."

"Oh?" Lia felt the heat in her cheeks, and turned so that he couldn't see, pulling out her phone from her backpack. "Yeah, same."

He glanced over to Gem and smiled when they rolled their eyes. "What are you doing tonight?"

"I'm not sure yet. Why?" Lia asked.

"Oh." Devon swallowed and blinked, an odd look settling over his face. "Wow. I thought you would be busy."

He mimed shooting a water gun at her, and she shrugged.

"So," he said slowly. "Between lessons and rehearsal, I'm going to be trapped with my violin forever. I have been trapped. I never even had time to really think about how to do this."

"Yes," Lia said, glancing at their hands. "Your crowded high school agenda."

"Don't laugh. I can't even find my agenda. Who knows where I'm supposed to be now?" He laughed and ducked, hair falling over his eyes. "Do you want to come to orchestra rehearsal? You can watch. No one minds. People do it all the time, and you don't have to stay for all of it if it's boring. We could just spend some more time together during break and after."

Lia exhaled through her nose, chest tight with joy. "Are we dating?"

"We probably have to go on a date to do that."

She would've sworn he blushed.

"So . . ." Gem studied their nails.

He definitely blushed then. "You can stay, too. Do homework or chat or nap. It feels safer to be near you two."

Gem and Lia agreed to stay. It would be nice to put off going home, and Lia wanted to figure out who her assassin was without her mom looming over her shoulder. Gem and Lia picked a corner near the back of the auditorium, where the heat puffed out of a vent at random intervals and the overhead light didn't flicker, and a dozen other friends picked uncomfortable wooden seats around them. Lia scrolled through her spreadsheet of everyone's schedules. At least fifteen were theoretically free when Lia and Gem had seen the figure at the park.

"Aubree, Bryce, Cassidy, Devon, Hunter, Jax, Jeremiah, Laurie, Mateo, Mercedes, Nicky, Noah, Oliver, Ryder, Rose, Stephen, Tamora, and Zack," Lia said. "Plus anyone whose schedule changed since the game started."

"Who even is Aubree?" Gem asked, scrolling through their phone.

"Transferred last year. Loves Hello Kitty." Lia groaned. "I had way more information in my journal."

Lia reached down into her bag to grab her agenda, and left half of her textbooks on the floor.

Gem snorted and glanced down. "Well, well, well." Gem reached into Lia's backpack and pulled a small leather journal from the very bottom. "Someone named Lia Prince is the worst."

"What the hell?" Lia took her journal from Gem and flipped through it. It was a bit beaten up, as if it had been living at the bottom of a bag for weeks, but she had emptied her backpack at home the day she thought it was gone. "No way."

The pages were as Lia remembered them, and a cold dread settled over her. Had she really missed this? Forgotten she had grabbed it?

"It was not in there this whole time," she said. "It couldn't have been. I emptied this bag so many times."

Gem nodded, eyes wide. "Yeah."

"I did!"

"I am sure you did," Gem said. "Just like I am sure that trauma can affect memory."

Lia's fingers picked at the fraying leather strings meant to keep the journal shut, and flipped open the journal to Aubree's page.

"Afraid of dogs and bees," read Lia. "Great. My memory is terrible, our friends are dead, and someone I can't figure out is going to take me out of the game."

Lia drew a line through everyone on the football and soccer teams. They had withdrawn and forfeited their upcoming matches.

"Not to be a broken record," Gem said, "but priorities. Mark off Ryder. He was tutoring. I can't imagine Laurie getting her hands dirty, Jax is creepy but was on a date, and Mateo was streaming League all afternoon. His streaming schedule is in his bio."

Lia sank down into her seat and propped her feet up on the chair in front of her. "Okay, that helps."

They lapsed into silence. Lia watched the rehearsal, in awe of the way the players shifted from students to musicians. Devon tilted his chin and arched his fingers, preparing to play, and the tension seeped from him as the music carried across the auditorium. There was a purpose in the movement and calm in his face, and Lia couldn't think of a time when she had ever felt how he looked. But still a sense of calm settled over her as Devon and the others played on. The instructor called for them to stop and spoke to the horn section. Devon lowered his violin.

He caught her gaze every time he could, the crook of his smile lost in the stage lights.

Gem groaned. "I'm going to run to Sonic and you can moon over Devon while I'm gone."

"You're still in the game and there is a literal murderer running around," Lia pointed out. "I should go with you."

"If you go with me, we won't be let back into the school." Gem raised one hand to Lia's face. "I love you, and I understand your fear; however, I need a minute or two alone to eat jalapeño poppers in my car with no one to judge me."

"I only judge you when you eat all of them before I can have one," Lia said.

"And . . . well . . . I'm going to talk to May."

Lia's face fell. "Oh."

"Yeah, she said she wanted to talk, and I don't really want to do that with an audience," Gem said, their smile slipping. "I'll text you when I get to my car, when I get to Sonic, and when I get back. There's this stairwell right behind the stage. I should get back during their first break, and you can let me in through there."

"You'll lock the car, right?" Lia asked.

"Of course," Gem said. "And Mr. Jackson is almost always on his porch right now, so it's not like I'll be alone."

The man who had lived across from the school for the last decade was practically a volunteer security guard for the parking lots at this point, but to get to the car, Gem would have to walk down the street. They wouldn't be on school property.

"I'll be fine," Gem said. "I'll be on the phone with May for most of the time. Don't worry."

Lia tried not to worry. She really did. She waved at Devon from her spot in the back of the auditorium and focused on her homework. Gem texted twice as promised, and when Gem was in the lot and about to walk back, Lia slipped out of her row. Devon glanced at Lia as she climbed onto the stage.

"Gem went to Sonic and is out back now," Lia explained. "Is there some sort of secret door back here?"

"Oh, yeah." He grabbed his water bottle and led her to a crooked metal door behind the curtain on stage right. "This leads to that back lot but the door locks automatically, so you can open it but don't let it close behind you."

Lia peeked over the edge of the stairs down into the dim hall. The back lot was a swathe of cracked concrete between the school and a neighboring housing community, and it wasn't technically school grounds. Most students used it when they arrived too late to find a spot in the student lots. "Creepy. I never knew this was here."

"We use it to leave," Devon said, tapping the graffiti-covered cement walls. "And keep it a secret so no one catches us skipping."

Lia snorted. "Like you ever have. Thanks."

"Just save me a tater tot or something," Devon said.

OMW, Lia sent Gem. She jogged down the stairs and opened the door. No Gem. She checked her phone—nothing.

Lia propped open the door to the back lot with a rock. The area was mostly empty, only a few people lingering on porches and in driveways. Lia sprinted to the lot.

Gem's car sat empty and off in the middle of the lot.

And Gem, unmoving, sat propped up against its side.

Lia froze. Hot, sticky fear prickled over her skin and clogged her throat. There was no one else around, and no reason why Gem would ever sit on the ground. Lia forced one leg forward. Then the other.

"Gem?" she called, voice shaking. The hair stood up straight on Lia's arms.

"I messed up," shouted Gem. "I'm out."

"Gem," Lia croaked. "What the heck?"

"I got tagged and my leggings are wet. If I stand up, it'll look like I peed myself." Gem stared up at Lia. "What's up?"

Lia let out a strangled laugh. "I thought you were dead."

"Crap. I'm sorry."

Lia sank down next to Gem, still laughing. Gem snorted. "Is it really that funny?"

"No," Lia said, gasping for breath. "But you're not dead, so . . ."

"I was foolish!" Gem gasped and swooned, lying across Lia's legs. "They have killed me mother. Run away, I pray you!"

"Okay, calm down, Macbeth." Lia hugged Gem tightly, then pushed them off. "You're getting me all wet."

"It was Nelson Zook, and his water gun's tank was basically a bucket," Gem told her. "Macduff's son, actually."

"I only watched the play because you were in it." Lia stood and helped Gem up. "Let's go, Macduff."

CHAPTER 22

Lia delivered Devon a few tater tots, then left, removing the rock from the door and rejoining Gem in the car. Lia let Devon know that Gem was out

Bold of them to do it so close to school, Devon texted as Gem drove Lia home. **Get home safe.**

You too, Lia said. **It was a good excuse to get together while it lasted at least.**

We don't need an excuse to get together.

Lia grinned and tucked her phone away. "It wasn't Nelson the other day, you know."

Nelson was a stout kid with lanky brown hair and a love of neon hoodies. His family had lived and died in Lincoln for over a century. The tradition must have run too deep in his family for him to quit even with the ban.

"Yeah, our park stalker was too tall," Gem said.

Lia turned her phone over and over in her hands. "I wonder how many people withdrew."

There was no way to know how many people were still playing, but Lia was convinced there were definitely more than Devon, Lia, and Nelson still in the game.

If Nelson was willing to get Gem so close to school, maybe her assassin—Aubree, Bryce, Cassidy, Devon, Hunter, Jeremiah, Mercedes, Nicky, Noah, Oliver, Rose, Stephen, Tamora, Zack, or someone else she hadn't considered—was too.

"Can you drop me off at the corner?" Lia asked as they turned onto her street. "I want to walk around the block."

Gem stared at her. "Alone?"

"Hardly." Lia gestured to the handful of people getting home, checking the mail, and walking after work. "I have an hour and a half before sunset, and I'll be three blocks away. I just want to see how closely my assassin is watching me."

Gem stopped the car a driveway over from Lia's house. From there, Lia could see her father through the kitchen window making coffee. He was already in his after-work clothes—a sweatshirt from Mark's college and cheap joggers. He used to make coffee for Mark when he left early on weekends to play Assassins. He had listened to Mark's strategies. It wasn't the same, of course. Mark was a good student, and playing had been a reward. Even before Abby, her father hadn't been thrilled about her playing.

"Is he being weird?" Gem asked, following her line of sight. "I swear, we had two friends die, and if he's bugging you about your grades, I will—"

"He's being okay," Lia said. "I would rather deal with my assassin over him right now."

He wasn't being anything. It was like he was trying to pretend it wasn't happening, like Lia was too much of a bother.

"Do you have a plan?" Gem pulled out and drove past Lia's

house. Three blocks away, at the entrance to their neighborhood, Gem pulled over again. "I could stay."

"No, go change clothes," Lia said. "I'll just walk slow enough for him to be out of the kitchen and figure out if my assassin is hanging around."

"Be careful." Gem unlocked the car door. "And text me when you get home."

Gem lingered at the stoplight for a moment after they drove off. Lia waved to them, her phone in hand just in case. Her water gun was hidden in the front pocket of her coat, and she searched the yards and streets around her. No shadowy figures lurked behind trash cans or cars. Only a few squirrels paid attention to her.

So Lia walked, one hand holding her phone as if she were busy but her eyes darting left and right with each step. A few neighbors waved. Several dogs barked. No one approached.

"So much for assassins," she whispered, texting Gem as she paused at the corner before her house. **I'm fine. Don't worry. No shadowy stalker.**

Lia turned to head home. At the far end of her street, in the dark foliage of a privacy hedge, two spots like binocular lenses glinted. Lia swallowed and carried on walking straight past her street. She pulled her hood up around the back of her neck, but not high enough to block the edges of her sight. If they followed, she would need a new plan.

At the next corner, she paused and twisted around, pretending to crack her back. No one followed.

Lia continued down the street, and at the next corner where the street ended, a lone figure stood one block away to her left. A hood covered their face, and the evening light made them nothing more than a silhouette. They must have cut through backyards and smaller streets. The only identifiable thing about them was the way their hood bunched up at the back. Hair in a bun?

Lia had three choices then: turn around and head back, turn left and face them, or turn right and see how intent they were on following her.

She turned right and didn't look back. Cars passed on the street, keeping her safe if this were part of the game.

If it wasn't, then there wasn't much that could keep her safe. At least she was in a populated place. Unlike Ben, she wasn't alone in the dark. She glanced over her shoulder.

No one there.

The next corner was a three-way stop with one road leading to a small neighborhood pool that was closed and one leading back toward Lia's house. She was a good five-minute walk from home now. A car turned in front of her. A shadow skittered behind it.

There, the figure knelt near a parked car. In their hand was what had to be a water gun.

Who was it? Too tall for Aubree or Rose or Zack. Lia's mind was spinning. And whoever it was, was fast. They must have been running to keep up with Lia through the backyards.

And it meant they were either herding her toward the pool or egging her on into a head-on confrontation.

Lia backtracked. She jogged, and by the time she hit the turn she had come from, the figure was there, in the distance, blocking her path. They wanted her near the pool, then.

Her phone vibrated as she backtracked yet again.

It was Devon.

Is Gem home safe and dry?

Lia texted him back, glancing behind her after each word.

Yes. I am walking the last few blocks home

Her phone rang.

"Hello?" she asked, and tried to keep the soft thrill of his instant response out of her voice.

"Do you have no sense of self-preservation?" Devon said. Someone spoke over him. Lia couldn't make out the words. "Yes. Yes. I know. Lia, where are you?"

"I told you," she said. "I'm walking home. I wanted to walk for a minute, so Gem dropped me off at the entrance to the neighborhood. It was only three blocks."

"Good." He sighed. "No, wait. What do you mean 'was'?"

Lia hesitated at the edge of the small park that was little more than a four-car lot, drained and covered pool, and little grassy area with concrete tables and benches. At the far edge of the park was a short drop-off shadowed by trees and a tall house. A dirt path encircled the whole area with one little fork leading out of the neighborhood. It was a shortcut to the next housing development.

If Lia took it, she would be near Abby's house, and if she carried on over the trail, she would be in the park where Abby died.

"The other day there was someone spying on Gem and me at the park," Lia whispered into the phone. "Pretty sure it was my assassin. And now, today, I saw them when I was nearly home, so I tried to go a different way. They keep trying to cut me off. I figure they want me someplace quieter."

The chain-link fence around the pool creaked in the wind, metal rattling against metal, and Lia looked back.

Between her and the exit stood the figure. Here, they looked taller than they had on the streets and the other day with Gem. Maybe it was how close they suddenly were. Maybe it was the way their shoulders didn't slump as they moved.

No, as they stalked.

"You went someplace quieter, didn't you?" Devon's voice dropped until the static of their connection nearly drowned it out. "Lia, where are you?"

She picked up her pace and put the pool between her and her assassin. Her phone shook against her ear.

Her assassin tucked their empty hands into their hoodie pocket, and Lia pulled out her water gun. Goose bumps prickled across her arms.

"The Pine Valley pool," she said. "But it's fine. I have a water gun."

"That is not what I'm worried about." A door on Devon's end slammed, and Lia jumped. "It's a game, Lia. Just let them shoot you. This stress isn't worth whatever it is you want."

But it was. Recognition, acceptance, understanding—it would all be hers if she won the game.

And she could win it. Because she understood it.

Winning it was something she could achieve. There was nothing else in Lincoln for her.

Footsteps crunched over gravel. Her assassin darted around the corner of the pool. Lia ripped her arm up and fired once. Water splattered against her assassin's neck, soaking the front of their hoodie, and they doubled over. Lia sprinted down the path and toward the trees. She skidded to a stop at the edge of the park, far out of range for her assassin to shoot.

"I got them," she said to Devon before shouting, "You're out, whoever you are. Good show. Who do I tell the Council I got?"

Her assassin didn't answer. They raised their head and followed. Lia stepped back.

A ding rang in her ears and Devon asked, "Why would you do that?"

"Why would I do what?" Lia huffed. Her assassin was too lithe to be Cassidy and far faster than Stephen. They leapt over one of the benches and headed straight toward her. "I'm too busy to be doing anything."

Her assassin started sprinting toward her. Lia's hand tightened around her water gun.

"Hang on," Devon said. A car started. "Where are you now?"

Lia raised her arm again, panic trembling through her, and aimed for her assassin's face. It was rude, but they hadn't stopped. Why hadn't they stopped?

"You're out!" She fired once and missed. "Just tell me who you are so I can send the email."

Still, they said nothing.

"Where are you now?" Devon's voice shook.

Lia fired again, and her assassin shrieked and rubbed their eyes. "You know that path through Pine Valley that connects to the big walking park in Pleasant Pines? I'll be there."

His response was lost in the rattle of her phone as she ran.

"They didn't stop." Lia took off down the path, out of her neighborhood. Her phone smacked her ear with every stride. "They were out, but they didn't stop."

There was no reason for them to do that.

"Didn't stop what?" Devon asked, voice reverberating with the dead giveaway of speakerphone.

"I shot them," Lia said with a gasp. Her calves burned. She could hear nothing but her heart and Devon's voice over the sounds of her feet slapping against the dirt. "They kept coming after me instead of exchanging info with me for the Council."

"Are you kidding me?" Devon asked. He was cursing now.

Lia had never heard him curse, and the laughter stuttered out of her. She was, except for whoever was after her, utterly alone.

And this was not part of the game.

CHAPTER 23

Lia burst out of the path and into Pleasant Pine Park as tires squealed in the parking lot. The path behind her was dark and lonely, overhanging branches keeping her from seeing too far. The black SUV in the lot turned off, and Devon jumped out. She glanced back. No one had followed her.

That she could see.

"What were you doing?" he shouted. "I really don't care if you play, but I am not going to be part of some weird mind game."

"I have no idea what you're talking about," she said, gasping. The stitch in her side ached, and the wind chilled the sweat coating her skin. Her backpack straps cut into her arms. "I'm the one being mind-gamed."

"Come on." He hooked one arm around her waist and helped her to the car, his fingers tight against her ribs. "Please tell me you didn't really run the whole way."

Lia shook her head. "Then I shall tell you nothing."

He practically lifted her into the passenger seat of his mom's car and buckled the seat belt for her before she could protest.

Devon locked the car as soon as he was in it. "This is getting dangerous, Lia," he said, fiddling with the strings of his hoodie. She'd never seen him in one, and he looked smaller with the fleece hood pulled up around the back of his neck like a scarf. "And I'm tired of your weird messages and calls and the game."

"What messages?" Lia asked, confused. "We were texting, and you're the one who got weird and called me."

"You're walking alone where—" He rolled his eyes. "You emailed me."

"I did not," Lia said. "Why would I email you? We were already talking."

He stared at her, eyes sweeping from her muddy shoes to the tangle of her hair. "You emailed me a picture."

"No," she said slowly, as if she were talking to a small child. "I was busy, and even if I wanted to send you a message, I'd text it. I'm not an animal."

"We need to talk," he said. "Is it okay if we go to my house? My dad's there, so he can call your mom, but we can talk in my room."

Lia nodded. "Sure. Okay. I'll just tell my mom we needed to talk." She closed her eyes and leaned back against the seat, her breathing evening out.

"Why did you run to the park?" Devon asked, eyes on the road and hands too tight on the wheel.

Lia rubbed her cheeks. The cold had started to fade, but still they stung. "There wasn't really anywhere else to go. The person following kept lapping me when I was walking down the street, so they were definitely faster than me. I would've had to run in a half circle to get out of the park, and they would've caught up with me in three steps. So I just ran."

"To Pleasant Pines?" he asked.

"To the only place at the other end of the path." She shuddered. "They should have stopped. I shot them. By the rules, they're out, and we needed to swap information. But they just kept following me. I don't know. You were listening."

"Yeah, but what if they were just approaching you to talk?" He glanced at her as he turned onto his street and winced. "And then you ran?"

"They said nothing, stalked toward me, and never took their hood off," she said. "If they were going to talk to me, there were less creepy ways to do it."

"True." He parked his mom's car in the driveway and touched Lia's chin. His thumb ran down her cheek. "You're bleeding."

"What?" She touched her cheek. A few specks of blood dotted her fingers. "It must have been a branch while I was running. The closest I got to the person was ten feet."

He sighed, shoulders slumping. "And you hit them at ten feet?"

"Oh no," Lia said, and grinned. "They were much farther away when I shot them. It was very impressive."

"Of course it was." His hand tapped against her jaw, and then very quickly he leaned in and kissed her cheek. "Come on."

Lia had never been inside Devon's house. She grabbed his hand as they went inside, her cold fingers lacing through his warm ones. He didn't shake her off, but his shoulders tensed. The house was warm and crowded; an old hutch next to the door was organized with baskets for keys and mail. He let her pass so that he could lock the door behind her. The short entry hall opened up into a big living area on the left and a wide, bright dining room on the right. Devon nudged her toward the dining room. The table was littered with half-finished puzzles and a game of Scrabble. There was no room to eat at it.

"Who's winning?" Lia asked.

Devon laughed. "My dad. My dad always wins."

"No bonus points for sucking up," called his dad through the wide doorway connecting the dining room and kitchen. "Hello, Lia."

Devon pulled his hand away from Lia.

"Hi, Mr. Diaz," Lia said, waving slightly. "Do you need any help?"

"No, but thank you," he said with a smile. He was a tall man with white streaks in the black hair near his ears, and he had the same warm brown eyes as Devon. The cutting board before him was full of chopped chorizo, peppers, and apples, and he set the knife aside before wiping his hands on a rag. His bushy eyebrows furrowed. "Are you all right?"

Lia touched her cheek. "Yes, thanks. A tree branch disagreed with me walking near it."

"We're going to talk for a little bit," Devon said. He turned and glanced at Lia. "Do you want anything to drink?"

"No, I'm good." Lia looked around, the butter-yellow walls decorated with recipes and pictures, and she smiled at the sideways writing on the opposite door where they had tracked Devon's and his older sister Adriana's heights. "Thank you."

His dad cleared his throat. "Feel free to sit in the living room."

"I figured we could go up to my room since—"

"You can sit in the living room," Devon's dad said. He swept one arm toward the door. "Or you can stand in here and help with dinner."

Lia chuckled. Devon ducked his head, probably rolling his eyes. The pair sat side by side on an old green couch covered with two throw blankets, and Devon sat with his hands in his lap. Lia caught his dad peeking at them from around the corner.

"So," she said, "you think I emailed you?"

He brought his legs up onto the couch and turned to her. "You did email me. Pretending like you don't know about it isn't funny."

"I don't know a lot of things, and it isn't pretending." All the joy Lia felt at sitting in his house and seeing him so relaxed, so unlike he ever was around other people, faded. "That's not possible."

Her journal and now this—her memory might have been spotty from grief, but she hadn't emailed Devon.

"Who even emails?" she asked when Devon only stared at her. "I haven't emailed you. I'm not a teacher."

"Tons of terrible stuff has happened, and you're basically staring more terrifying stuff in the face," he said, pulling out his phone and scrolling through an impossibly long thread of emails. "And then you sent me this."

"I definitely didn't send you anything." But she took his phone anyway and opened the file. There was no subject or body to the email. Only the picture. "And I don't see why it would—"

It was a picture of a figure, back to the camera, in the park. It was a far better look at them than Lia had gotten in person— they weren't as tall as Lia had thought, their hair was bunched up under their hood, and the water gun in their hand was a delicate shade of blush pink. Behind them was one of the cement lunch tables.

"They were following me," Lia said. "But this isn't who I shot. I was never behind them."

The person near the pool had been taller. Lia was sure of it. Their hood had been pulled tight around their head, and they had carried nothing. Even here, safe in Devon's house, their empty hands felt far more dangerous than any water gun could. Lia looked at the email.

"The person I shot at the park, the one who wouldn't talk," she said, "that was the one who scared me. This was just the one I saw following me, and I was never close enough to either for pictures."

"You shouldn't have been walking around alone at all." He knotted and unknotted the strings of his hoodie. "And you sent that to me. It's your email."

"But I didn't!" Despite the warmth of the house, she shivered. "What do the other emails say?"

"You tell me," he said, handing over his phone again.

There was an email from after she left with Gem.

> Devon, I can't shake it. Something's wrong with me.
> I keep seeing people following me. I'm trying to just
> focus on the game, and it's infuriating. It's so easy
> to stay alive, and all these idiots are just squandering
> their chances, going out alone and trying to hide in
> plain sight like they're some sort of ninja. I'm tired of
> it. If they try to take me out, they're in for a terrible
> surprise.

"This wasn't me," she whispered. "When would I ever say *squandering*?"

Devon shrugged. "Check your sent folder."

"Of course." Lia practically tossed his phone and pulled up hers. There were over a dozen emails from her to Devon, and none of them she recognized.

"'Devon, Ben's out. Idiot. I told him not to go anywhere alone, and I won't let him ruin this for me.'" She shook her head. "I would never have called Ben an idiot."

"But you sent me this," he said. "I'm really not okay with playing games, Lia. You sent me these, and you never took my advice."

"What was your advice?" she asked, pulling up one of his responses.

He had offered to come sit with her. There were paragraphs of text, things she didn't know and things she did. Devon had sent her little puzzles and riddles, and he had offered to visit her at her house. The responses sounded like things she would say, but they were off. She had declined to meet him at her house, and he had said no to meeting at the park. He had confided in her. Told her he wanted to quit music.

And her response—or rather, the response from whoever was pretending to be her: "You can't quit. Music is so useful."

Lia stared at him for a moment and set her phone down.

"Is that really what you think I would say?" she asked. Then she sighed. "Do you really want to quit music?"

He glanced at her, brows a squiggly line above his eyes. "Is that really important right now?"

"It's context," she said. "Do you?"

"Yes." He swallowed, eyes darting toward the kitchen, and nodded. "I don't love it anymore. It used to make me happy, but now it feels like a chore."

"Then you should quit," Lia said. She traced his fingers and leaned her forehead against his shoulder. "You should quit and find something that makes you happy. Just because it's useful doesn't mean you have to do it."

"Lia." He sighed and touched her face, her shoulder, her leg, as if to check to make sure she was still there. "What is going on?"

"I don't know." She sniffed and rubbed the small scratch on her cheek. "Maybe someone is trying to get me out of the game?"

"Ben is dead, Lia." He pulled back to look in her eyes, and his other hand came up to her face. "No one would kill over the game, or go through this much trouble over it."

"Ben has been dead," Lia said, "plenty of people were still playing, and I know for a fact I didn't send you these messages."

"Are you sure?" Devon pulled away from her when she scowled. "Okay, sorry. It's just that it's your email."

Lia reared back, discomfort prickling over her skin. "You don't believe me?"

"The last few weeks have been very hard," he said. "It's easy to forget things."

"I didn't forget having whole conversations with you." Lia rose and stepped away from the couch. Her shoes scuffed against the old wooden floors of his house. The sounds of his dad cooking stopped. "I didn't send those messages, and whoever you've been talking to wasn't me."

The evening jingle of the news undercut Lia's bitter whispering, and Devon rubbed his eyes.

"What's the simpler explanation?" he asked. "That you sent

me these messages and forgot, or that someone did what—hacked your email and has been leading me on for a week and a half for no discernible reason?"

The simplest explanation was that she was a fool, then.

"You don't know me at all," she whispered. "Not even a little bit."

And it hurt. No one got Lia. Gem did the most, but that was one person. Lia's parents barely tolerated her love of games and deep ambivalence to school and sports, the only two things they did understand. Her teachers certainly didn't get her, and for years Lia had built up this ideal in her mind. Devon Diaz—so smart and observant, he had to understand.

He couldn't tell her apart from someone's crappy idea of a joke.

Devon put his phone away and shook his head. He looked up at her.

"Hey, guys," his dad called from the kitchen. "Come in here for a moment."

Lia wasn't sure she could take anything else happening today, but Devon tugged her gently into the kitchen with one hand holding her sleeve. He didn't even touch her to do it.

She checked her Sent messages for other messages she hadn't been a part of and found one not to Devon but to the Council.

> The Council,
> Will Abby's death affect my standing if I continue playing?
> Sincerely,
> Lia Prince

The Council had never responded. It was such a bitter message to send. Lia never would have.

"Lia, I already talked to your mom. She's coming to get you," Devon's dad said. His laptop was balanced on top of a twelve-pack, and a muted news story played out behind him. "Cassidy Clarke died this afternoon."

Lia grabbed ahold of the kitchen counter. She felt like she might pass out.

"What?" One of Devon's hands twitched toward her, but he wrapped his arms around himself instead. "Our Cassidy?"

His dad nodded and laid one hand on his shoulder. "Yeah. Lia, I know you're probably not okay, but your mom will be here in a few minutes to get you."

"When . . . when did it happen?" Lia asked.

"A few hours ago I think." He nodded. "Unfortunately, the news got there first, so if anyone sends either of you anything, it's probably better not to look at it."

Lia turned her phone off.

"Where was she?" Devon asked, staring at Lia.

She had seen too many crime shows to ignore his tone. She had been in that park twenty minutes ago.

He was thinking that maybe she had something to do with it.

"Pine Valley." His dad sighed. "So definitely no more walking alone or sudden drives to get friends."

Devon's face fell and he opened his mouth, but the doorbell was ringing and a rushing sound was filling Lia's ears, everything around her fading out until all she could think about was how Lincoln was so cursed that the news was just hanging around for the next dead kid.

Abby. Ben. Cassidy. Abby. Ben. Cassidy. Abby. Ben.

"Cassidy," her mother's voice said from the front door. "What a tragedy."

That stalker at the park hadn't been part of the game, and now Cassidy was dead. She shuddered. Devon grabbed her hand before she could follow his dad to the door.

"I was just worried," he whispered. "That could've been you instead of Cassidy. I wasn't saying you had anything to do with it."

But it felt like someone was. It felt like a lot of things had been leading to this, and Lia had only just been told she was losing a game she hadn't been told she was playing. There was too much that didn't make sense for it just to be that she couldn't remember things. She knew who she was and what she was doing. She did.

Lia walked slowly to the car. There was an odd pinch to her mom's face that kept her from looking at Lia. Once they were both buckled in and on the road, Lia screenshot all the messages, her photo folders without the photo sent to Devon, and the history of devices that had been using her email account.

"We need to stop by the police station before we go home," her mom said. "To talk about Abby and Ben again now that Cassidy . . ."

Lia nodded, texted Devon her device history, and said, "Yeah, I figured."

An iPhone in Lincoln, AR, with an IP that definitely wasn't her.

"Just answer their questions," her mom said. "It'll be okay."

Lia only nodded again. There wasn't much she could say. There wasn't much she could think. She sent a single message to the Council before she could rethink it.

Why didn't you respond to that email?

Either the Council had a blanket policy not to respond to nonstandard questions, or—

A text from a restricted number popped up on her phone.

Why would we respond to someone not in the game?

CHAPTER 24

Cassidy was all over social media, even though the news couldn't report her name since she was a minor at seventeen.

Past tense was beginning to make Lia sick.

"They just want to talk with you since you knew everyone," her mom said, fixing Lia's hair and holding out her nice coat. She must have grabbed it before leaving the house. She must have known they wanted to talk to Lia before Cassidy's death was even on the official news and not just Twitter. "What happened to your face?"

"Tree branch I ran past," she said. "So that's great."

"Just answer their questions," said her mom. "Don't be smart. Don't tell them more than they ask. I'll be in there with you."

As they parked, Lia shoved her bag into the back of the car. There was nothing in there to help her. If anything, her journal made her look absurd. She had stalked her classmates, and now someone was killing them. She had been one of the last to see Ben and one of the people to find him, and now she had been alone— for all she could prove—in the park where Cassidy was killed.

Abby looked even worse.

Would Gem and Devon simply blame trauma for Lia forgetting she murdered two people?

God, they all thought Lia had killed people.

The police station was crowded when they arrived. A few people lingered on the sidewalk, checking phones and pictures on big, professional cameras. A cop met them at their car and escorted them in, keeping their body between Lia and the street, and they were led through a back door. Lia swallowed, sinking into a chair as they were told to wait. Her mom sat with her.

"Is Dad coming?" Lia asked.

"No," her mom said, "he's looking into something else."

They made Lia wait. It was at least thirty minutes after she sat down before a tall white man she vaguely recognized as Detective James came to greet them. He had spoken to Lia after Ben's death.

"Mrs. Prince, Lia, thank you for waiting. Come on in here," he said, leading them into a small conference room and shutting the door behind them. He pulled out a chair for Lia and gestured to one for her mom. He was in a wrinkled suit that might've been the one he had been wearing last time Lia saw him, but this time he didn't pull at the knot of his tie. "How are you, Lia?"

"I'm okay, I think," she said. "Thanks."

Three dead—two times Lia had been there and one time she hadn't.

"As you probably know, another of your classmates was found a little while ago," he said, and set his elbows on the table. "Cassidy Clarke. Did you know her?"

"Yeah." Lia took a breath. "She sat in front of me in a few classes, and she's been in a few more since freshman year."

"But you didn't know her well?" he asked.

The room was off-white and bare, and the soft sound of her

mom's breath rumbled in Lia's ear. There was nothing in there to look at except James. She didn't have anything to do with Cassidy's death, but her heart hammered away anyway.

"No, she was in choir and she was really good in history." Lia shrugged and crossed her arms, shoving her shaking hands underneath them. "She just got the Governor's Scholarship. She was really happy about it."

Detective James nodded. "Her parents mentioned that. They also mentioned a game that the seniors play in secret. A game about killing each other."

"Assassins," Lia said. It wasn't really a secret. The students just liked pretending it was and that they were mysterious killers. "She was. Most people in Lincoln have played it."

"It's why you were following Abby the morning she died, right?" he asked.

"Yeah, she was my team's first target," she said.

"Have you remembered anything else since we spoke last?" He jotted something down on his notebook, his gaze never quite finding hers. The way his wrinkles and beard trembled as he spoke kept his expression unreadable. "Anything at all that might be helpful?"

The back of her neck prickled, and her stomach rolled. She felt exactly as she had in the park, watching the shadowy figure watch her, except now there were emails on her phone she hadn't sent. There was a picture of someone she didn't know in her email. There were two people who had been following her.

She shook her head. "No, I'm sorry."

"You know, it's weird," the detective said, laughing softly and leaning back in his chair. "I've worked here for twenty years, and

I can't place you at all. Saw your brother Mark play in the state finals as a junior. I could pick him or Abby or Ben or Cassidy out of a crowd. You, though? There wasn't even gossip about you until you were found with Abby."

Lia picked at her shirtsleeves. "I've never really done anything worth remembering."

"No," he said, "you haven't."

He pulled a small folder out from under his notebook, the white edges of a photo fanning out from within it. He pulled it out to reveal a small pink water gun lying in the grass.

"I wasn't in Lincoln till a few years ago," he said, turning the photo so that she could see it right side up. "Folks talk about Assassins like it's real assassins, but most of it's harmless. All fun and games. Most of the people in that room out there played it. They said this was fairly usual—girl alone in a park with nothing but a water gun and flashlight after school. You have one, right?"

Lia nodded. "Mine's blue."

"Yeah, this was Cassidy's." The pink gun was identical to the one Lia had seen in that photo sent to Devon.

"You were pretty beaten up when you found Abby." His gaze darted to her cheek and then back to his folder. "Bruised knees, hands, and one bad one across your calves."

"I tripped," Lia said. "Like Abby."

"Which is weird since there was nothing to trip over." He pulled out another picture, this one of a small knife. It was the dull short kind that came with a full set of silverware in fancy lunch boxes. A few people at school used them. They only just passed the "no knives" rule because they were no more dangerous than the plastic ones in the cafeteria. "Do you recognize this?"

"No," Lia said, even though she could think of only one reason for why he would ask.

He laid another two photos before her, this time one of a tree, where a thin circle of bark had been worn away from the trunk. The other was of a pale, battered leg, which was marred by a narrow red line across the shin. "At least, there was nothing to trip over when we got there, but it was just you and Abby in Pleasant Pines."

The back of Lia's throat grew hot and damp. Her mouth watered. She whispered, "Is that her leg?"

"You had tried to take her out the day before, hadn't you?" he asked. "But you missed, she got hurt, and it almost got the game canceled. It was you who convinced Principal White not to ban it."

Lia closed her eyes.

"And Ben Barnard, bless him, got taken out of the game right before he was killed." Pages rustled, and a photo slid across the metal table. "According to friends, he got shot in the hand."

Lia shook her head. "I saw his hand. I can't see it again. I don't want to see it again. Please take it away."

"How did you cut your cheek?" he asked.

"I was running," she said. "From my assassin. They chased after me when Gem dropped me off at home."

Her mom sucked in a breath. "You were supposed to stop playing."

"Everyone was, but you didn't," said James. "And you were running through Pleasant Pines, right? Near Pine Valley pool?"

"I was on the phone with Devon," Lia said. "I didn't see Cassidy at all."

"You sent him a picture, too. You didn't just talk to him."

Lia opened her eyes, and James covered up Ben's picture with a different one. Cassidy, face hidden by her hood, splayed out in the grass next to one of the cement tables near Pine Valley pool. Red stained the corner of the table. The pink water gun lay in the grass next to her. Lia gagged.

"No . . . no, Cassidy wasn't there when I was there," Lia said, stammering. "There was this other person following me, and I shot them, but they didn't stop to exchange information. We're supposed to exchange information when we get a kill, but they just kept following me, so I ran. Cassidy wasn't there. There wasn't anyone else there."

"You took them out?" he asked. He was far too calm for this. Three people were dead, and Lia was sure if she opened her mouth again, nothing but screaming would come out. "Are you sure Cassidy didn't take you out?"

This time the picture he put before her was a printout of a single email. Lia had been Cassidy's target.

"You take the game pretty seriously. That's what everyone said when we talked to them after Ben. He was, too, but you were obsessed. You followed everyone you thought would play all last year and made a little journal, didn't you? You wrote down their schedules, their fears, their friends. You stalked your whole class," said James. "I don't get the game. It's tradition, sure, but that's more than anyone else. Even the guys out there said they didn't go that hard. But you did. You wanted to win. You didn't want to be forgettable, hidden in your older brother's shadow anymore, did you? Abby, Ben, Cassidy—they were all high achievers. You're just Lia Prince, and you were jealous."

And it was all true and terrible, but Lia shook her head.

"This game is a way for you to finally get recognized," he said, "but Abby, Ben, and Cassidy were going to ruin that for you. Three kids with achievements taking away the only thing you had."

"No."

She wanted to be noticed. God, no one realized how much invisibility hurt. If she were a terrible daughter, at least her parents might pay attention to her, but being mediocre was worse. Too good to need help, too bad to need attention. Her parents, her teachers, her friends—no one ever paid attention to just her.

"You set up a trip wire for Abby." James gathered his photos and tucked them away. "You went back to Ben's and took out your anger on him, and when you found him the next day, you contaminated the scene to explain away anything we might find. Cassidy assassinated you in the game, but you couldn't let her get away with that."

"No," Lia said again. "And I can prove it."

She knew it went against every episode of *Law & Order* she had ever seen, but she pulled out her phone.

"Lia!" Her mom grabbed her arm, and Lia shook her off.

"No, look. I didn't send any of those messages to Devon. The IP address they came from in my account isn't my phone. That photo was taken with someone else's phone." Lia scrolled through her messages and opened the one from the restricted number. "Even the Council for Assassins knew those emails weren't me. I wanted to win the game, but they were my friends. I never hurt any of them."

Abby Ascher. Ben Barnard. Cassidy Clarke.

That was a lie. They hadn't been her friends, but they deserved real justice. All the shows and movies said killers stuck their noses into investigations, but Lia had been tossed into this one.

"I didn't hurt any of them," she said. "I didn't even have my journal until today. Someone stole it from our biology room."

And it had her email address right there on the front page.

"But you have it now?" James asked, his face hard. "Convenient."

People had been doing it for ages. Lia had even copied and pasted the roster directly into the journal and then crossed off the names of those she figured weren't playing. The list was glued onto the first few pages.

"I'm not the only one who does it," she said. "I even—"

"That's enough." Lia's mom dropped her hand on the table. "We're done. Are you arresting her?"

A chill oozed down Lia's spine.

"No—" said James, and Lia's mom interrupted him.

"Then I'm taking Lia home, where she will stay." Her fingers found Lia's arm and pulled her up. "If you wish to speak with her again, please contact our lawyer. My husband has just arrived and should have that information for you should it be necessary. We're leaving."

They did let her go. Lia's thoughts were jumbled, her ears full of that same rushing again. They weren't keeping her. They could have kept her, she was pretty sure. They had to know that you could trace the origin of photos. They had to know she didn't kill Abby, Ben, and Cassidy.

Devon and Gem had to know that.

Lia's mom sat her in the backseat of the car and crawled in there with her. She buckled Lia in. Her fingers shook, and it took four tries before she got the seat belt into the clip. Lia pulled out her phone.

"I wish you hadn't done that," her mom whispered.

"I didn't send those emails," Lia said. "Even the Council knew it."

Her mom shook her head. "Lia, do you even know who you're taking orders from for this stupid game?"

She didn't. The Council was the Council. There was always one, and they were always anonymous.

Lia scrolled through the list of Assassins participant schedules she kept on her phone. Abby wasn't even in this version, but she would've been first. Instead, Ben was, followed by Eric Bins. Cassidy was third on Lia's list.

Her mom said nothing else. Her father didn't talk to her either. They talked over her on the drive home. They talked about lawyers and costs, Mark potentially coming back and missing out on class, and Lia being suspended from school. Her mom dragged her from the car to her bedroom. Lia sat on her bed.

"Lia," she said softly, kneeling in front of her and holding her hands. "I won't be angry. I just need to know."

Lia's stomach clenched. "You should know."

"I should," her mom said, "so please tell me."

"No, I mean you should know me well enough by now." Lia pulled away. "What do you think happened?"

"Lia," her mom said sharply. "I do not want to play one of your games right now."

"This isn't a game. Even if it were, you have never played any of my games. You don't even know if I'm a murderer? You don't know me well enough to know the answer to that? You would never even think Mark would kill anyone, but you have to ask me?" Lia tugged at her hair, her sleeves, anything she could hold that wouldn't put up a fight. "I heard him say it. Mark's your favorite. Of course he is. The words made all those little things real, and now this."

"That's not true. Lia, you are our daughter, and we love you." Her mom went out into the hall and waved for her father to come. Lia could feel the "but" at the end of that sentence building up in her chest. "We know this Assassins game was important to you, but it's just a stupid game, and you're throwing—"

"It wasn't a stupid game when Mark almost won!" Lia leapt to her feet. The anger welled up in her so fast and hot that she couldn't breathe deep enough to speak. There weren't any words left for what she was feeling. There were too many words she wanted to say. It all burst out of her in a shriek.

Lia slammed her bedroom door shut and locked it with a trembling hand. She slid to the floor.

An hour later, when the words came back and her hands stopped shaking too badly for her to write, she slipped a note under the door.

I didn't.

And it hurt that she even had to say it.

CHAPTER 25

She wasn't going to school. It was a command passed on through the door of her room. Lia hadn't expected to even leave the house, and Thursday had gone on so long that the very thought of waking up and facing her classmates made her nauseous. Lia's potential involvement in the deaths settled over the house like a fine dust all of them were desperate not to disturb, and Lia only left her room to eat when her parents threatened to take the door off of its hinges. It was bound to be worse if she went to school, and she wasn't even sure she could. Everyone must have known she had been interrogated. Maybe Devon had told more people by now.

There were a dozen official emails, tweets, and Facebook posts, none of which Lia read. They wouldn't say more than the gossip. Cassidy's name hadn't been released by the police but by the neighbors who posted it online the moment they saw the cops. Lia couldn't deal with what they were possibly saying about her.

But it should've been easy to prove she wasn't the killer. Cop shows did it all the time with phone records and subpoenas for email accounts.

After dinner, she crawled into bed with her journal and her phone—how long until they took all her things and picked through her life piece by piece? Her phone had been off since they spoke to James.

Lia powered on her phone and turned it facedown on the bed. It vibrated with notifications for a full minute.

"Okay," she said, and took a deep breath. "Okay. Someone is killing my classmates."

There was no denying it. As much as Abby's death had seemed accidental and Ben's could've been a one-off, it was clear all three were connected. Those messages, too, tied Lia to the murders.

"Why me?" she asked, flipping open her journal. "Why frame me?"

That was the only reason she could see for those messages. They made her seem obsessed, more than she was, and like she was forgetting major things when she denied sending them. She almost couldn't blame Devon for being worried.

Almost.

The first page of her journal was the class roster. Lia erased the line she had drawn through Abby's name when she figured Abby wouldn't play.

Abby Ascher: covered up as an accident during a run by someone who knew her favorite paths to take.

Lia checked her phone. Fifty-two missed messages. She opened the only message Gem had sent.

Don't check ANYTHING. Call me.

She called, and the phone rang as she ran down the rest of the list.

Ben Barnard: attacked at his house and the hand he was tagged out with brutalized.

"Lia!" Gem's voice was a hoarse whisper. "Are you okay?"

"So I guess my name is already in everyone's mouth?" Lia asked.

Eric Bins: totally fine and not a part of this at all.

Gem groaned. "Sort of. Mostly because everyone knew you were playing and then someone saw you. How are you?"

Gem didn't even pretend to dance around the question of "did you do it?" They knew.

Lia leaned back against her headboard and pulled her knees up to her chest. "My mom asked me if I killed them."

Gem hissed.

"Devon apparently has been talking to someone pretending to be me," Lia said. "No clue what to do about that or why or who it is other than it must obviously be the killer because you don't have two weird things happening at once.

"I was at the park where they found Cassidy." Lia pulled her journal onto the top of her knees. "Someone chased me there, and I was on the phone with Devon. Surely that'll be enough to prove it wasn't me?"

Cassidy Clarke: head wound in the park while stalking Lia.

"I'm the only thing that ties the deaths together." Lia traced a line around each name—Ascher, Barnard, Clarke. "Cassidy was my assassin."

"Jeez," whispered Gem. "You are the common thread."

"So either I'm a serial killer and I forgot all about it," Lia said while Gem hemmed and hawed over the phone, "or there is a serial killer trying to frame me."

"Don't they usually start with small things, though?" Gem

said. "I barely have my life together. Don't tell me someone in our class has already worked their way up to killing us *and* being able to frame someone."

Lia erased the line she had drawn through Devon's name, too. "Well, I sure as hell don't have my life together enough to do all this."

The game tied her to each of the dead, and something, like a word on the tip of her tongue, stuck in her mind. She stared at her journal, couldn't think of it, and tossed the book aside.

"Get some sleep," Gem said. "I think you've earned it, and maybe it will all have blown over by tomorrow."

It did not blow over by the time Lia woke up an hour before noon. She rolled out of bed, shuffling through the house in her pajamas. Her mom was in the kitchen, and her father was at work. Her mom made her eat at the table, and Lia managed a few spoons of cereal before she remembered the blood caught in the pitted cement of the picnic table where Cassidy had died. If she stared long enough at her cereal, they looked the same. She retreated to her room for the rest of the day.

No one from the football team is here, Gem texted her at lunch. The table they eat at is empty, and Peter yelled at some freshmen when they tried to sit there. Devon's here, though, and he is out of it. I don't think he's heard a word anyone has said.

Great, Lia texted Gem back. **Sad and thinks his not-girlfriend is a serial killer.**

IDK it seems more "everything sucks" than specifically I KISSED A KILLER, you know? He's been chewing the same bite of his sandwich for like three minutes.

Gem sent her a picture: Devon at a table with Faith, Georgia, and Mateo. Devon stared off into space, a sandwich in one hand,

and Mateo stole his chips. Faith struggled to cut the chicken in her homemade salad with a fork. Georgia reading instead of eating. A few seconds later, Gem called her.

"Hello?" Lia said. All she could hear was the rumble of the cafeteria.

"Hey, Devon," Gem said. "Have you talked to Lia?"

"I heard the police talked to her yesterday," said Faith. "Is that true?"

"I don't know anything," Devon said quickly. "I don't have my phone."

God, did he turn it over to the cops, or were his parents just worried?

"She is super obsessed with Assassins," said Faith, and there came a sound like her teeth clinking against metal. "I knew playing that game was a bad idea."

Devon said nothing, and Georgia snorted.

"Like not playing would've helped," she said. "It's Lia. Lia obsesses. It's what she does. Unless they arrest her, I doubt it was her."

Lia sighed. That was comforting at least.

"Still," mumbled Faith. "It's weird."

"I don't want to talk about this," Devon said quickly. "Gem, can I talk to you?"

And Gem hung up. Lia sat on her bed, flipping through her journal and ignoring her phone until another text message came.

He wants to talk to you, Gem said, but his parents took his phone and he has orchestra tonight. So I don't think he thinks you're a murderer.

Small mercies.

CHAPTER 26

Lia told her mom she was going to take a nap after an early dinner. Her parents usually left her alone in the evening, and the last twenty-four hours seemed like they would be the same. Her mom didn't even check on her for the hours after lunch until knocking on her door around five. She said Lia had to eat, and Lia agreed. She played along, and she played nicely. They had to think she was doing what they wanted.

When she was confident they were distracted by a movie, Lia crawled out her bedroom window. She hated biking, but it would have to do. The school was a thirty-minute ride away, and Lia could wait for someone to leave through that back door, and she could slip in when they did. She was chilled with sweat by the time she got there. Her leggings and hoodie stuck to her skin.

Across the street, Mr. Jackson was sitting on his porch smoking, and he waved at Lia. Lia raised one hand in return.

Her plan worked; the moment the door opened, a few kids shoved a rock against the door so they could slip back in. Lia darted up the stairs once the group left. Devon was still in his chair, a bottle of water between his knees and his head thrown back. The people around him were talking amongst themselves in a group a ways off. Lia crept out of the stairwell.

"Devon?" she half whispered.

He jerked up. "What?"

Lia waved and nodded to the stairs.

"What are you doing here?" he asked, glancing around.

"Gem said you wanted to talk." Lia backed up till she was against the door. "I can leave if you want."

Devon glanced at the stage where the instructor and security guards were talking. "Okay, sure, yeah. That's fine."

It would've been better if he didn't sound so unsure.

"Great," she said, and made her way to the stairwell. "I should probably leave before break is over, but I wanted to talk to you."

"Please tell me you didn't walk here or something equally as dangerous?" he asked, leaning back against the railing.

They stopped a story above the door, far enough from either to hear it open but not be in the way of anyone coming or going.

"Does that mean you don't think I'm a murderer?" she asked.

"Of course I don't think you're a murderer," Devon said, shaking his head. His hair fell over his eyes. "The emails are still bizarre, but no offense, in no world can I picture you fighting Ben or Cassidy and winning."

She could hardly take offense at being called not a killer.

"Full offense taken at you not believing me about the emails." Lia leaned against the opposite wall. "I told the cops about them, which was probably a bad move if someone is framing me."

"Is someone framing you?" he asked. "Is that not a leap?"

"If not, it's the deadliest string of coincidences ever." She knocked his knee with hers. "You looked scared when I left your house, and you didn't say anything after that."

He scowled. "Detective James called my parents and asked me tons of questions about you. They are panicked."

"I've made an excellent first impression, then." Lia sighed. "I should've stuck to science fair." She had never won science fair either, but at least no one died during it.

"I always liked watching you do science fair."

Lia shook her head. "Why? It's so boring."

"Yeah, but you put on a show," he said. "You spent one whole judging round talking about the etymology of 'sinister' when you did that chirality project."

Lia flushed and mumbled, "It was a chemistry project, and I got no points that round."

"And it was the most I've ever learned during science fair. It was great." He laughed softly and shook his head. "I like that when you know something, you know you know it. You're in a different category each year, and each year you know exactly what you're talking about. I could goof my way through a bunch of biology experiments, but you go all in. Like with Assassins. You don't do things by halves. It's a little intimidating."

Lia had never thought of herself as intimidating. Off-putting maybe, but she was short, plain, and blunt. Her dad called her a jack-of-all-trades and master of none. There was nothing she truly excelled at unless researching counted.

"You like me because I'm intimidating?" she asked.

"I like you for a lot of reasons," he said. "Maybe that's a strong word. You're certain? You know what you know? You trust yourself?"

Lia wasn't sure she trusted herself now, with the memories of her dead classmates' ghosts haunting her every thought. She didn't know what she was doing after high school. She didn't know how to carry on with Assassins when people were really turning up dead. She didn't know how to navigate this weird new life she had found herself in.

She knew Devon, though.

"I don't feel like I can right now." Lia reached out and brushed his hair back. He caught her hand with his, and she didn't pull away. "I didn't send you those emails, but other weird things have happened. I found my journal in my backpack the other day, even though it can't have been in there. I emptied it out completely when I thought I had lost the journal. It's mesh. You can't lose things in it. I was right. There was a second person at that park with Cassidy and me. I didn't shoot Cassidy. I—"

And she couldn't say it because the idea that she had been right there, she had been steps from the person who slammed Cassidy's head against a table hard enough to kill her, burned the words out of her. Devon tugged her against his chest and wrapped his arms around her shoulders. Lia tucked her face into his neck.

"It's okay," he whispered. "We'll be okay."

A hand reached over the railing and yanked Devon back. Lia grabbed his arms. The hand pulled his jacket harder.

His feet lifted off the ground. The rush of blood in her ears drowned out Devon's shriek, his fingers gripping the rail as his jacket sleeves cut into his shoulders. Lia wrapped one arm around his waist and shoved one of the sleeves down his arm and off.

"Let go!" she cried out.

Devon let go of the rail with both hands and let his arms dangle. Lia hugged him to her. The jacket ripped off of him. It fluttered to the landing below. Footsteps thundered down the stairs.

Lia took off after them. She jumped the last three stairs of the landing and skidded into the wall. A figure, all in black, darted down the last landing. Lia leapt after them.

If Devon had fallen, it would've looked like Lia had pushed him.

The attacker smacked into the door. It flew open, and they sprinted out. Lia raced after, following their path in the dim light of the streetlamps. They turned left, back toward the school, and took the path leading into the neighborhood around the school. Lia had mapped the area outside of the school grounds extensively for the game, and she took a path that would intercept theirs. She ran without thinking, eyes on the corner ahead. One right, and she would have them. Distantly, Devon screamed her name. She took the corner at full speed.

The figure stood in front of her, water gun raised. It was the same person from the park. Their face was covered by the folds of a thin black scarf, and they were taller than Lia by half a foot. Their white tennis shoes were immaculate despite the mud.

"Why?" Lia asked.

She could fight them. Water was nothing compared to what they had done.

They cocked their head to the side and shot her point-blank in the face.

Lia collapsed, gasping. Water burned in her eyes, dripping down her nose and into her open mouth. She tried to stand and gagged. It wasn't just water. She couldn't see.

Footsteps paced around her. Lia scrambled back, eyes shut and gravel ripping into her hands. A shout echoed down the alley.

Devon screamed. Lia's vision cleared just enough for her to see the dark smear of her attacker flee.

By the time she had heaved up the water she had inhaled and Devon had tried to wipe the water mixture from her eyes, the attacker was gone.

CHAPTER 27

"It wasn't part of the game!" Lia wrung the towel the cops had pulled from their trunk in her hands. The water had been laced with soap and some sort of pepper oil, and Devon had gotten another orchestra member to get some milk from the vending machine. Lia's face was still red and stinging. "They tried to kill Devon."

"He's fine," said a cop Lia hadn't met before and regretted meeting now. He had the countenance and facial hair of a thirteen-year-old shih tzu, and Lia liked him as much as she liked yappy dogs. He hadn't even asked what her name was. "That fall wouldn't have killed him, probably wouldn't have even broken a bone, and seems like it successfully lured you off of school property."

Behind his head, where Devon sat talking to his mom, Lia met Devon's eyes. He shook his head. He was wrapped in a blanket. He had taken off Lia's soaked jacket and replaced it with his button-down shirt, but now they were both cold and suffering.

"The game's banned. We get suspended if we play," Lia said.

"And we would get disqualified and arrested if we pushed some-one down the stairs just to win."

"Look," the cop said with a heavy sigh. "I know how y'all get with this game."

"How do you know it's not the person who killed Abby, Ben, and Cassidy?"

"You said it was a girl," he said.

"I said they were in leggings and a jacket with a scarf over their face," Lia said quickly. She had described every last detail she could remember, muttering them over and over to Devon so she wouldn't forget. "I don't know who they are."

Detective James stepped out of an old tan Caprice and zeroed in on Lia. She winced.

Here Lia was, at the center of a mess, again.

"But I have seen this person before," Lia said. Her sight was bleary now, but it hadn't been when she had turned that corner. "Yesterday someone chased me through the park. This person had the same silhouette and hood and everything."

"Okay," the cop said. "Describe the first figure."

Lia hadn't been close enough to compare her height with theirs, but she knew how tall the fence was. Weight was impos-sible to guess. Build was better. Their face had been hidden be-hind a black scarf, but a few strands of hair had poked out from beneath it.

"Between five four and five ten, slender and maybe athletic, brown hair that's at least shoulder length, a black cotton scarf, a pullover black hoodie, and solid white tennis shoes. The fancy wool kind. I don't know the name."

"Did anyone else happen to see them?" Detective James asked, coming to a stop right behind the cop.

"I think Devon did?" she said, but she was so unsure it came out as a question.

"I believe Mr. Diaz has already given his statement," the detective replied, "and as I recall it, you weren't supposed to go anywhere."

Lia rubbed the wet neck of her shirt. "I needed to talk to Devon."

"He is your boyfriend, right?" he asked.

Lia shrugged. She wasn't entirely sure how she would describe him, but the detective was staring at her with his unreadable eyes.

"Stop talking." Lia's mom pushed around James and grabbed Lia's arm. "I swear to God, Lia, not another word."

"Mrs. Prince," James said, "your—"

"Was cleared by the paramedics." Lia's mom tugged her toward the car, past Devon and his mom, and he raised his arms at Lia in question. "So we are leaving."

"Wait." Lia ripped her hand free. "I need to give Devon his shirt back."

Her mom's face got somehow stormier.

Lia made her way to Devon. "Bruised?" she asked.

"A little," he said. "I told them about the messages, stairs, and whoever attacked you. I think they thought you pushed me, and I was protecting you? No offense, but I would not do that."

"Yeah." Lia pulled his shirt from her shoulders and handed it back to him. "If I ever do that, feel free to push me back."

"I don't think they really listened to me." Devon's gaze darted to his mom, and then he leaned into Lia and cupped her face in his hands. He whispered, "They didn't leave after shooting you. They waited. I think they were trying to decide what else to do with you."

She shook out her hair, wet clothes sticking to her skin, and fought back another shudder. "They're probably not done with you either."

They probably weren't only going to pull him off the railing. The water gun and spiked water were insurance.

"Keep it." Devon wrapped his shirt around Lia's shoulders. "You should probably be in a car."

It was nice to have someone's attention solely on her. Devon had held back her hair while she had heaved up a lungful of water, and Lia's mom still hadn't asked if she was okay, only urged her to leave. It wasn't winter anymore, but it was dark and windy, and the cold had sunk into Lia's bones.

"I feel like a burrito," she said.

"You look like a burrito." He rubbed her shoulders. "A cold, soggy burrito."

His lips, rolled together, twitched. Lia laughed.

"That cop called you my boyfriend," she said softly. "We just haven't talked about it and—"

His chest rumbled with laughter, and he patted her arm. "I know we probably should talk about that, but can we talk about it after all this is over and we're not in the middle of three death investigations?"

"Yeah," she mumbled, and pulled away. "Of course."

He squeezed her hands. "It's just this is a lot and if someone is trying to kill me, then—"

"Lia!" Her mom broke away from where she was talking with the cops and James, and approached them.

Devon's mom waylaid her with a hand on her arm, and Devon pulled away from Lia.

"You didn't send any of those messages, did you?" he asked.

Lia shook her head. "Whoever was emailing you is probably the one who killed Cassidy."

"It's weird," Devon said. "I was always next to Cass in lines. We used to play tic-tac-toe on the school assembly schedules."

Cassidy Clarke and Devon Diaz—they were right next to each other alphabetically.

"Hello, Lia." Dr. Diaz, Devon's mom, walked over. "Thank you for not letting Devon fall off a flight of stairs."

Devon had inherited her height and sharp features, but her brown skin was a shade darker and warmer and her black hair cut short in a perfect bob. It looked lovely against her red coat and white scarf.

Very aware of the damp hair stuck to her face and how her mascara must have run, Lia only nodded and said, "Of course."

Such an offhanded comment, but it was the key to all of it. This was what Lia couldn't think of when staring at the roster in her journal and erasing their scratched-out names. The deaths were in the order of the class list, just like her journal had been. Ascher, Barnard, Clarke, and Diaz.

"You were always next, Devon," she said. "It's your names." She was going to say more, but her mom, expression tense, started walking toward them again. Devon let his mom lead him to her car, and Lia braced herself for her mom's wrath. She stopped before Lia, taking her in.

"What happened now?" her mom asked. "You couldn't wait until this had all blown over?"

As if Lia were the cause of the problems, no questions asked. She got no benefit of the doubt. She got dealt with.

"Devon might have died," Lia said, "and you want that to blow over?"

"We told you to stay home. We told you to withdraw from the game," she said. "This is serious, Lia. This is a police investigation. Children are dead, and you're running around like nothing has changed."

"It wasn't part of the game!" Lia said, her shivering slurring her words. "I had to talk to him, and then someone attacked him."

Her mom's shoulders slumped. She reached out as if to hug Lia and instead rubbed her shoulder. "You are very lucky that Devon and Mr. Jackson both saw the person who did it when you chased them out."

Mr. Jackson was worth five school security guards.

"They'll try to kill Devon again," Lia said. "Detective James gets that, right?"

"Lia." Her mother sighed and unlocked the car. "There is a murderer on the loose. They're not going to waste their time playing pranks on you."

But they sure did waste a lot of time emailing Devon and pretending to be Lia.

CHAPTER 28

When they got home, Lia's mom had a metal lockbox on the kitchen counter. Inside was Lia's phone, laptop, Switch, bike lock key, and house keys. Her mom shut and locked it all in the box in front of her.

"What are you doing?" Lia asked. "I need to talk to Devon."

"You talked to Devon." Her mom's jaw tightened. "You snuck out of the house against our orders and the police, and you nearly got Devon killed. You're done talking."

"I saved him!" she protested.

"People are dead, Lia! You are not a hero. I'm tired of your obsession with Assassins. It's done." She grabbed Lia's arm and yanked her down the hall. "Abby Ascher was murdered in this neighborhood. What were you thinking biking that far alone?"

Lia dug her heels into the carpet, dragging them to a stop right outside her door. "I know Abby's dead. I know where she died. I know how she died. I know what she sounded like as she died and what she looked like after. I know how happy Ben was the night before he died, and I know how still he was the next day. My friends are dead. You can't expect me to not do anything!"

Her mom paused in the bright light of the hallway, her hair stuck to her lips and mud trailing behind her shoes. "One thing, Lia. We have asked you to do one thing."

"You never asked me to do anything," whispered Lia. "The cops said don't go anywhere, and they meant don't leave town. And I haven't."

"You always pick apart things until you find what you think is a loophole," her mom said, shaking her head. "You're not as smart as you think you are. Sometimes you just have to do as asked."

"I've always done what you've asked." Lia yanked her arm away. "I gave up debate. I gave up piano. I gave up Latin for Spanish. I have done everything you asked and nothing I wanted. All those AP classes you made me take—I hate them. All those tutors and competitions? I did those because you asked."

"That isn't fair, Lia," her mom said. "That was for you. For your own good."

"No, I wasn't good enough for you!" Lia shouted. "What I liked wasn't good enough for you."

Her mom was silent for a moment. "We'll talk in the morning," she said quietly. "They're canceling school after Monday until this is dealt with. Monday, I will drop you off, and I will pick you up. You will stay at home. You will do the homework they give you. You can have your things back when you stop acting like a child."

After her mom left, Lia tore through her old dresser picking through frayed cables and broken keyboards. "Aha!" She pulled out an old flip phone. The charger tumbled out with it. "Come on. Come on."

The old phone powered on. Lia scrolled through the options,

each screen taking an age to load. She had no cell service, but it would still connect to Wi-Fi. Lia typed in the password, messing up every other letter on the number pad. The loading signal kept loading.

"Lights out!" her mom shouted through the door.

Lia turned off the light. The phone connected, and she crawled into bed with it in one hand and her Assassins journal in the other. It took another five minutes to get to a chat screen on the HTML free page no one used anymore. She sent a single message to the group chat they had made for their Assassins' team. Ben's icon stayed shadowed and silent, but she liked the idea that their words still reached some part of him.

What do they all have in common? Lia asked the chat.

It took three minutes to send.

Gem's response was instant. YOU DIDN'T TELL ME YOU GOT INTERROGATED AS A SUSPECT AND THEN SNUCK OUT OF YOUR HOUSE FOR A DATE?

Lia winced.

It wasn't a date, Devon said. Someone has been sending me emails from Lia's account and pretending to be her

They even emailed the Council, Lia said. She tapped the keys and sank deeper beneath her blanket. **The Council knew it wasn't me, though. How?**

Ellipses danced next to Devon's name. Three dead students, all related to Lia, and a series of emails that make her sound like she's becoming a bit too obsessed with the game. This is too much for it not to be related. In another town, maybe three students would die in one month, but this is Lincoln. We didn't have that many students to begin with

Lia glanced out her bedroom window, never more aware that her one-story home was so vulnerable. Anyone could reach her window. **But Detective James didn't seem like he thought we were lying, right?**

No. Especially since we have other witnesses

Let's go over it then, Devon said, and Lia imagined him—glasses slipping down his nose, hair in disarray as he ran his hand through his hair. Tonight felt way too personal to be just about the game.

So, Lia said, **why kill Abby Ascher, Ben Barnard, and Cassidy Clarke?**

She underlined their names in her journal and skipped Eric Bins.

You said I was next, Devon typed slowly, each word showing up a few seconds after the other. So someone is killing people in alphabetical order with matching initials?

Serial killers do weird things, Gem said.

Eric Bins is between Ben Barnard and Cassidy Clarke, but it would be a huge coincidence for it to go alphabetically after tonight. Lia scratched out Eric's name. After Devon was Andrew Doyle, Kaitlyn Eames, and Emma Earl. **Maybe you four did something to them? And who's Emma Earl?**

Georgia. She goes by her middle name, said Gem. Someone could've been jealous of Abby and Cass, but Ben was aggressively nice. No way someone wanted revenge against him.

Abby and Cass had just gotten the Governor's Scholarship like I did, Devon said, but Ben hadn't

Lia turned to a fresh page of her journal and wrote down *A. Ascher, B. Barnard, C. Clarke,* and *D. Diaz.* The pen spun in her hand, and she added one last name.

E. Earl.

May got the scholarship. Gem sent a screenshot of a conversation. She found out a few weeks ago, but she's deferring for a year. Her scholarship slot is going to the next in line.

The names were the strongest link, but Eric Bins interrupted it. The scholarship connection was weak, and May had only told Gem after Ben's death. How would anyone have known who got it early? It was like when Lia had tried to bake pumpkin pie at Christmas but forgot eggs; she was missing something and without it, nothing would set. She shook her head.

I mean, I sort of get killing over a full ride, Gem said finally. Especially for legacy students. It's bragging rights, room and board, and no worry in the back of your mind about what comes next.

Gem, how is May? Lia typed.

She just wants to talk about Ben. Gem went silent for a moment. Whoever did this is a monster.

A monster who knows a terrifying amount about us, Devon said. Our schedules, our plans . . . they even know Lia snuck out tonight to meet me.

Lia swallowed and typed the words she had been dreading. **If you had fallen over the railing, it would've looked like I pushed you. They're setting me up. And they're definitely watching me.**

Neither of them responded.

They're probably the one who stole my journal, Lia said, flipping through the pages. **That's how they knew everyone's schedules and that Ben was allergic to latex.**

They're smart enough to plan and escape the cops, Gem said, but not smart enough to realize they won't get the scholarship this way.

Lia hesitated. **If they're going to frame me, that breaks the alphabet trend, and I'm not in line for the scholarship. I'm nowhere close. Why me?**

No offense, but more pressing—this means they're in our biology class. That's what this means, right? Gem asked. And if they're canceling school, kids will be home alone all day. They'll be vulnerable.

Lia closed her Assassins journal and looked toward her dark window. Was the killer watching her now? **My mom is dropping me off and picking me up. I've got no phone or computer.**

How are you talking to us now? Devon asked.

Old flip phone on Wi-Fi.

Lia got up and wedged three pencils into the sliding window to keep it shut just in case the lock was picked. She pulled the blinds shut.

We stop this now, Lia said. **No more sitting ducks. Tomorrow we go after them.**

CHAPTER 29

Lia didn't go to sleep immediately. She sent an email to the Council.

> How did you know it wasn't me, and why didn't you say anything?

Their response didn't come until Sunday morning.

> We do not interfere in the lives of civilians no matter how dastardly they may be. Lincoln leaves us alone to do as we may, so we leave Lincoln alone to do as it may.

Which didn't really help.

Lia's mother dropped her off at school Monday one minute before the first bell rang. Devon and Gem were waiting on the sidewalk near the drop-off, and Lia's mom said nothing when Lia said goodbye. Surely she wasn't really a suspect now if Detective James was letting her go to school, but that meant they had no clue who it actually was. If today didn't work, things would get worse. Lia wouldn't let anything happen to Devon or anyone else.

No matter what.

"How are you doing?" she asked Devon.

Devon leaned in and kissed her cheek. "I've been better."

"I made a list." Lia pulled out her journal and held it out to Gem. "I narrowed it down to seven people in our biology class who aren't playing the game. The Council didn't give me anything new."

The seven the Council might have meant were Sam Douglas, Krystal Fowler, Hannah Henry, Faith Franklin, Suzanna Smith, Penny Peterson, and Jessica Thompson

"You can add Mateo, even though I hate to say it," Gem said. "He withdrew before that email was sent."

Lia added him, but it was hard to picture Mateo killing anyone. It was hard to picture *anyone* she knew as a killer.

Lia looked around at the kids milling about. Maybe they were wrong. Maybe it wasn't even a senior or a student. It was too late for that now. At least they were safe at school. She had barely slept the night before. There were too many thoughts in her mind. "Time to sit in biology and hope the killer isn't in there."

"I hope they are," Devon muttered. "I want this over."

They made their way to Ms. Christie's class. Only she was in there that early, the first bell still a few minutes away. Devon, Gem, and Lia took seats in the very back, and Ms. Christie handed them a packet outlining what would be happening over the next few weeks. After today, school was canceled for a week to give everyone time to grieve and the police time to find the killer.

If the cancellation lasted longer, the school had prepared another packet to send out to students by email. How bleak for everyone to be prepared for weeks of a murderer carrying on. Lia didn't read the whole sheet.

They would end this today.

"We have to leave our bags and phones in homeroom during lunch," Devon said. "That's annoying."

Gem turned the first page over. "Is orchestra still meeting tonight?"

"We are," Devon said, "but only for a few minutes to vote on what we want to do about the spring concert and rehearsals."

"Maybe we should steal the key to homeroom so we can come back during lunch and go through bags," Lia whispered. She mapped out where everyone was sitting in the back of her journal and circled the eight they needed to investigate. "Serial killers keep trophies. Maybe they'll have one, and if not, maybe they left my account open on their phone."

It would be hard to unlock the phones but not impossible. Probably. Whoever the killer was had guessed Lia's password. How hard could it be?

"Okay, second idea: we ask Ms. Christie if we can do some work in here during lunch," Gem said. "She'll still have to leave to heat up her food and supervise the start of lunch like she always does, and she's not going to say no to us."

"She won't?" Lia asked.

Gem sighed. "You're so used to your parents saying no that you dismiss the idea of asking adults for help entirely."

Devon leaned over Lia's shoulder, one hand on her arm. "I'll do it. She won't say no to me."

"Do it at the end of class," Lia said. Her hunt for schedules last semester had taught her that people were more likely to agree to something simple if they wanted to leave quickly.

The other students began to trickle into class after the first bell rang. Hannah and Penny were first, taking their seats in the middle row in somber silence, and Mateo, in a hoodie and sweatpants instead of his normal ugly sweater, nodded to Devon as he slipped into his seat a few desks over from Devon. Faith stopped at Ms. Christie's desk as she entered and took two of the handouts. She wore gray leggings and a red University of Arkansas fitted T-shirt. Her black tennis shoes looked new.

"Georgia's sick," Hannah said. "Her mom said it looks like food poisoning."

Lia glanced at Gem and mouthed, "Poisoning?"

Maybe the killer was stepping out of their comfort zone of blitz attacks and trip wires.

They shrugged.

The rest of the students on Lia's list wandered in right before the tardy bell, Suzanna out of breath and Sam cracking a smile as he skidded into class just as it rang. He caught sight of Abby's and Georgia's empty seats and winced. Faith patted his arm as he passed.

"She's just at home," she said. "No reason not to focus on school."

Hannah nodded. "She'll be fine."

Faith hummed, and Sam dropped his backpack next to his desk, collapsing into his seat. God, they were all falling apart one by one. The killer had screwed up everything.

Class went by far more slowly than it ever had. They didn't

study biology so much as write down what they might need for the final once school was back in session, and most of the class was devoted to talking about the cancellation. Faith was terrified the cancellation would affect college admissions, and Hannah was afraid no one would get to walk at graduation. No one seemed to have heard about Lia's failed chase at least. At the end of class, once everyone else had left and Ms. Christie was about to stand, Devon cleared his throat.

"Ms. Christie?" Devon asked, approaching her desk. "Is there any way we could stay here during lunch?" He gestured to Lia and Gem at the back of the room. "I know it's a lot to ask, but lunch is when people keep asking questions."

Devon's voice wavered a touch, and Lia's fingers tensed. She had tried so hard not to think about the empty spaces around them or the questions Devon and Gem might have faced when she wasn't at school.

"It's just a lot, you know?" Gem said from next to Lia. "And your class is near our third block class."

Ms. Christie took a deep breath. "If I let you stay in here, you have to clean up after yourselves."

"Of course," Devon said. "Yes, thank you. Thank you so much."

By the time lunch had arrived, the school halls were buzzing with news of Georgia's absence and bets on if the school would shut down for the rest of the semester. Devon wrapped one arm around Lia's waist to stop her from tackling Sam, whose bet had involved one more death.

"If it's not him," she whispered to Devon, "I'm still punching him."

He squeezed her and let go. "Let me buy you some brass knuckles first."

"Now," Ms. Christie said once they reached her room and the other students had dropped off their bags in their chairs and left. "You three sit in your normal seats and relax and I will be back in five minutes."

She vanished out the door with her lunch tote.

"See?" Gem said, heading for the bags. "Ask and you shall receive."

They went down the rows methodically, going through the students' bags, searching for something, anything, that would connect to the crimes.

Two minutes in and none of them had found anything useful.

Lia opened a bag without looking at whose it was and pulled out several neatly organized journals. "You know high school is too much when we need three agendas for one year."

Gem snorted.

Lia flipped through the first one and her head swam at the multicolored bullet points and to-do lists. She slid it back into place, the bag was impeccably packed with little pouches to keep everything private and neat, and she pulled out the next journal. This one was a butter-soft letter notebook tied shut with leather strips, and Lia was struck by the winding way the bow was tied. The first page of the journal was only a contact page, the upper right corner slightly bent. Lia turned it over.

Abby's name decorated the top of the first page. Next to it was a pale blue box filled in, the edges meticulously lined so that none of the ink bled through. Lia ran a hand down the page.

· *morning runs through Pleasant Pines w/Omelet*
· *breaks on bridge for 5 minutes*
· *1st target for assassination is Mark Crooks (?)*
· *Δ route (?)*

The page was full of notes. Lia turned to the next page, fingers shaking.

"Hey, Devon, the little triangle means change, right?" Lia asked, even though she knew the answer.

He checked his watch and put a phone back into the bag he was searching. "Yeah. Why?"

Lia nodded.

Ben's name was at the top of the second page, and beneath it in the jagged caps of Lia's own handwriting was "ALLERGIC TO LATEX; EPIPEN IN POCKET." The EpiPen note had been whited out, and beneath it was a color-coded copy of Ben's daily schedule from Lia's Assassins journal. Next to it a smaller copy of May's schedule, from her soccer practices to her weekend sleepovers with her best friend, had been taped neatly into the journal and the cut edges covered with "do it today!" and alarm clock stickers. A purple box had been filled in next to his name. A few notes lined the margins in looping cursive.

Lia turned the journal sideways to read "stays with team after practice to carpool" and "rxn appears 5–10m after exposure."

Fear settled heavy and cold at the base of Lia's spine, and she sat down on the floor next to the bag. Devon paused.

"Lia?" he asked.

"Two minutes left," Gem said. "What are you doing?"

She turned to the next page. Cassidy's schedule had been

carefully printed and pasted into the book as well, and the notes jotted down in cheerful yellow ink. An email address and password were highlighted at the top of the page. Next to them was a sticker in the shape of a lock. Another square, yellow, was next to her name.

"So organized," Lia whispered, flipping to the next page. "So meticulous."

Devon's name was handwritten at the top of the page in calligraphy and his schedule written out by hand. Lia had never followed him, and so none of his information was in her journal. Oxford-style notes took up the page; the left-hand side was an outline of things to cover in the emails to Devon. The bottom of the page included footnotes in miniscule cursive referring to his schedule and tendencies outlined on the page proper. *Garlic bread* was underlined in spring green. The box next to his name was empty.

"Check the phone in this bag," Lia said. "Now."

Gem rifled through the smaller pocket, unzipped a little leather pouch, and pulled out the phone. "We need the passcode."

"One minute." Devon tossed everything back into the bag and zipped it up. "Skip it."

"No," Lia said, "give it to me." She held it up and tilted it back until the oily surface was revealed, and four prints with little scratches from Faith's nail stared back at Lia.

"One, five, and zero," Lia said.

Devon winced and rifled through the rest of a bag. "I think that's eighty-one possible passcodes?"

"Thirty-six," Gem said quickly. "That's thirty-six possibilities if each one is used at least once and one is repeated."

"Work smarter, not harder," Lia whispered.

Even now, days later, Lia could remember the tone Faith had used when asking Lia about her test scores.

Lia typed in 1510 and the phone unlocked, revealing a home-page cordoned off into neat little squares full of apps. Lia opened the last-used mail app and found nothing. There were no emails to Devon.

She looked up the phone's IP address and locked the phone, putting it back into its pouch.

"Time," Devon said, closing the bag he was searching. "Lia, put it away."

She couldn't move. The scuff of Ms. Christie's Crocs echoed down the hall. Gem ripped the journal from Lia's trembling hands and returned it to the backpack. Devon darted down the aisles to make sure everything was in place, and the two of them took their seats. Lia lingered, standing, near her desk. She knew whose bag it was, but she checked her desk map to confirm whose seat it was anyway. Her finger traced the edges of the killer's name.

"I did everything right," Lia whispered. "I'm not sure why I didn't get higher. I earned it."

Devon stared at her, eyes wide, and the pencil in his grip snapped. Gem looked from him to Lia.

"What?" they asked.

"Lia?" Ms. Christie called from the door. "Is everything all right? You look frightened."

Lia turned to her. She felt light. She felt cold. She was completely unmoored from her body, and the words tumbled out of her in an awkward staccato. "I'm fine. Thank you. I just realized something I should have noticed earlier."

Her teacher nodded and sat at her desk. Lia crumpled up the

page of her journal and tossed it into the trash. She sat between Devon and Gem.

"You know who it is, don't you?" Gem asked quietly.

Devon nodded, and Lia opened up her Assassins journal. It was a taunt. Her knowledge had done this. Her drive to win had gotten her friends killed.

"She copied my journal and color-coded all the information she stole," whispered Lia. "Our lives are just footnotes to her."

CHAPTER 30

"They won't believe me," Lia said.

"Why?" Devon asked as they left Ms. Christie's room. "Why any of it?"

"Maybe the scholarship idea was right. Maybe she hated us all these years. Maybe she just likes killing." Lia walked through the hallway, her mind racing. "Does it matter? You're definitely next, and Georgia's in danger."

"And the cops thought we were just playing Assassins the other night." He paused outside of his third class of the day. "Great. Perfect. They definitely won't believe me if they didn't the first time."

"We have to stop her," Lia said. "She won't wait long enough for them to figure out who she is."

"It's such a bad plan," Gem said. "Of course she would get caught."

"Maybe the scholarship is her excuse," said Devon. "Maybe that's how she justified it. She's the most competitive person I know, and I know Lia."

Lia couldn't even bring herself to laugh. "Then why the alphabetical order?" she asked. "Why the pattern?"

Gem shrugged. "Who knows?"

Lia shook her head. "She's overplanning it—the bridge, Ben's allergy, stalking Cassidy, the stairwell. It's like she joined Assassins with a step-by-step plan to win before finding out the rules and her target. There were much easier ways to kill you."

"Comforting," Devon said. "I assume that means you think you can stop her?"

Lia nodded. "We need to out-plan the overplanner."

"We need to set a trap for her." Lia took Devon's hand, scared she would turn a corner later and find him dead. So long as he didn't leave her sight, it would be fine, but he had to leave her sight. "We can lure her out after school, as long as she thinks you're alone."

"She plans for days." Gem mimed writing in a journal. "She has color-coded bullet journals for each semester, makes lists upon lists of everything she needs to do, and uses stickers to mark her progress, but she never quite gets it all done. She spends all her time planning and then goes off-script. How do you trap that?"

"Even with Ben, which she clearly planned, it was a mess," Lia said. "And with Cassidy, she used what she had on hand. She didn't bring anything."

"If we get her into an empty room, she'll probably just try to strangle you," Gem said. "You can probably take her."

"No thank you," Devon said. "I prefer a bit more than 'probably' on my side, especially since she's been doing CrossFit."

She had overpowered the others. They couldn't risk that happening again. Lia let go of Devon and turned to Gem. "You should get that prop knife. Your fourth block is drama, right?"

Gem nodded. A junior glared at them as she shoved past Devon into class, and he squeezed Lia's hand.

"We have two minutes until the bell," he said, holding up his phone. "We can't clear a room of everything deadly before the end of school when her list of weapons includes a table."

"No, we give her several weapons that are too good for her to pass up but we make sure they can't actually hurt us," Lia whispered quickly. "Faith doesn't just think she's smarter than everyone but that she deserves everything. The world revolves around her. She won't even question a knife if we make sure it fits in with the surroundings at least a little. She's too self-centered to think it's out of place if it's for her."

"Go." Devon gave her a gentle shove. "Text me your plan. She's in my fourth-block class. You have until then."

Gem and Lia split up for third block, and Lia sat in the back of her communications class, her old flip phone barely keeping up with her typing. At least the school Wi-Fi was fast. Devon protested: he didn't want to die or get them hurt, but they all knew that if they even broached the topic of Faith Franklin being the killer that no one would believe them until evidence proved it. If Lia was right, and she was fairly sure she was, then Faith was getting desperate.

If this was a terrible plan to get the Governor's Scholarship, her deadline to be offered one was fast approaching, and Lia could almost understand that. Tuition, room and board, and school fees paid in full for four years—it was a dream many joked was worth killing for.

Lia texted Gem and Devon.

**If we're wrong and she's innocent, we'll all be fine.
If we're right, this will keep you safe and prove it's
her. Please trust me.**

No one ever believed Lia. No one ever had faith in her. No one ever trusted her.

But if she helped catch the killer and cleared her name, maybe the only gossip about her wouldn't be sordid rumors about murder and her obsession with Assassins.

Devon said:

> I do, and I should be the bait. If you're right, I'm next, and if it's Faith, I was one of her targets all along. She'll risk it to kill me. She already risked it the other night. The stairwell and Cassidy were way less organized.

Lia stared at Devon's words, her chest tight and eyes burning.

> **You'll be in danger.**
> Not if your plan works. I trust you
> **I'm tired of waking up only to find another friend dead. If no one else will face this head-on, we have to**

Gem texted:

> What do we do?

They decided that Devon would let it slip that he was going to be chilling in the drama room behind the stage before orchestra. They'd place a prop knife near the door so that Faith would see it. The one from *Wait Until Dark* would be perfect.

Lia knew Faith kept Mace on her keychain.

Gem, can you get rid of that?

Gem's response was slow.

Maybe? It's hard to rip something off of a keychain

Gem decided to try to get the Mace between third and fourth block while Lia distracted her. Lia would somehow distract Faith and let her know Devon would be alone and stop her before she could walk into fourth block.

Lia sprinted from the class once it was over. Students whispered and darted out of her way. Before Abby's death, Lia had been known in that way the laws of thermodynamics were—some students at Lincoln High knew of her and remembered her first name, but only a few knew her. Now everyone knew her.

She didn't like it.

Gem passed her near the corner by Faith's fourth block. Devon got there first, and Lia wrapped her fingers around his wrist, holding him back in the hallway.

"This isn't the plan?" he asked softly.

Lia leaned in close. "I need her to see us talking."

A carrot at the end of a stick wasn't enticing if the carrot wasn't supposed to be there in the first place. Traps needed context.

"Oh, okay," Devon said. "Think Gem can pull this off?"

"Yeah." Lia caught sight of Faith turning the far corner just behind Devon and smiled. "Slump your shoulders. Look tired."

"Be careful," she whispered, and patted his shoulder. He reached up to squeeze her hand. "Go inside and then meet me in the drama room the moment you can."

It was the only place to which they had access that would

make sure they were found. After twenty minutes, students would start wandering to the auditorium for rehearsal and Lia's mom would be looking for her from the pickup line.

Faith cut through the crowd toward the door next to Lia. Gem followed. Faith's keychain swung from her backpack zipper with each step, and Lia looked up. She let her mouth fall open slightly and waved. Faith stopped next to her.

"Lia," she said, her eyes flitting over her. "How are you?"

"You know." Lia shrugged and pretended it was hard to even force a smile. "I actually have a favor to ask you, but don't feel weird if you want to say no."

Faith cocked her head to the side, her long brown hair swinging forward in a sheet and suddenly all Lia could see was the barrel of Ben's water gun.

Lia realized her hands were clenched. She loosened them.

"Do you think I could borrow your copies of your sister's notes?" Lia asked, biting her nail. "Class has just been hard recently. I feel like an idiot. I didn't even think about asking for Mark's notes."

Even if she had, she was sure he wouldn't have handed them over.

Faith sighed, a slight smile on her lips. "Of course. We could meet after school today if you want?"

"Thank you so much." Lia threw her arms around Faith, hugged her tight for two seconds, and watched Gem finish unhooking the Mace canister from Faith's keychain. Lia squeezed Faith once more before letting go. "Really. That makes everything seem way less terrifying."

Gem pocketed the Mace and blended seamlessly into the crowded hallway.

"No problem," Faith said. "So today?"

"I can't. I'm staying for orchestra rehearsal with Devon. He usually decompresses backstage before everyone arrives, and I'm going to run and get some food before rehearsal starts." Lia shrugged and bit her lip. "Maybe tomorrow I can meet you somewhere?"

Faith smiled too broadly than anyone would on a day overshadowed by three deaths and nodded. "Tomorrow. I'll message you?"

"Sure!" Lia said. "Thanks again."

Lia made it to class with thirty seconds to spare. Everything felt so normal: her teacher went over a new chapter, her classmates looked over their homework they needed to do while school was canceled with bored expressions, and less studious kids played on their phones under desks and behind books. Lia messaged Devon to tell him what she had said, and he promised to try and mention it offhandedly if he thought he could. Lia was already halfway out the door when the bell rang. She raced to the auditorium. Gem was already there.

"Prop knife," Gem said, holding up a deceptively sharp switchblade. "Even has room for a squib at the end of the hilt. I'll keep her distracted for a minute so you have a chance to clear out anything else. I grabbed all the pens, pencils, and scissors. The tools are locked up, thankfully."

Lia swallowed, shuddering at the image of Devon beneath the blades of a circular saw.

Lia went over every inch of the room she could see and moved heavy, slammable objects to the far side of the room behind the teacher's desk. By the time Devon arrived, her hands were shaking. He dropped his bag in a desk chair and shut the door. She jumped.

"Sorry," he said. "Lia?"

"The papier-mâché masks aren't much of a threat, but you can throw them if need be." She moved to the side of the room where old books and props lined the wall. Lia tested their weight and opened an empty drawer. "She was strong enough to overpower Cassidy, so we—"

"Lia." He curled his hand around hers and closed the drawer. "It's okay."

"It's not." Lia spun, her nose bumping his chest. "It's really not."

"I trust you," he said.

Lia shuddered. "Why?"

"Because I've never known you to fail at something you put your mind to?" he said. "Because I know you'll be in here with me, and that makes me nervous, but everyone else was alone. Because I do. If you're asking me to analyze emotions, I need like five more hours and a nap."

Lia wrapped her arms around his waist and tucked her face into his shoulder. Devon's fingers tightened around hers. He kissed her cheek.

"We just have to make sure she's caught," he whispered. "We're at school. It's the middle of the day. If she really goes for this, she'll be desperate, but we know that. It'll be okay."

Lia sniffed and nodded. She pulled back. "Let's do this."

Lia picked up the knife. The knife was metal and rigid, and the give of the blade was barely noticeable when Lia poked it against her hand.

"Ouch." Devon took her hand and pulled the knife away before she could press it all the way down. "Not even pretend."

He set the fake knife on the shelf at the front of the room with other harmless props Lia had left there and took her hands. Lia kissed him quickly.

"One last thing," she said. "Can I borrow your phone?"

"Yeah."

Lia scrolled through his apps, settled on one, and tucked it against a shelf at the back of the room.

"All right," Devon said. "Let's get me murdered."

CHAPTER 31

Lia crouched under the teacher's desk in the back and watched the front of the room in the reflection of a display case. Devon laid his head on a desk as if he were napping. The door opened, Faith's reflection distorted. Devon startled.

"Hey!" Faith waved from the front of the room and grinned. "Do you have a minute? I have some notes for Lia and I know she's coming here later."

"Yeah, of course." Devon gestured to the empty seats. "What is it?"

She studied the shelf of old props. "Just some notes. You know her—a journal on Assassins but nothing for class."

Lia couldn't tell if she had picked up the knife.

"To be fair, it has been a rough month." His hand was a white-knuckled fist against his leg. "Have you heard back yet?"

"No, you know how it goes," Faith said, sighing and shrugging. One hand dropped into her pocket. "It must be nice to have everything taken care of already."

Devon laughed, and the sound rattled awkwardly out of his

tense mouth. "I suppose. It's a bit daunting. There are very strict guidelines for keeping the scholarship."

"I know." Faith walked to the back of the room, dragging her hand across each desk. She stopped across from Devon. "I thought you wanted to go out of state? Can you still? You should. I would."

If she took another step, Faith would see Lia in the reflection. Lia crept to her left, eyes on Faith's reflection in the glass. The other girl did nothing but stare at Devon.

"I already signed the paperwork," Devon said with ease, as if the words weren't the nails Faith needed to hammer his coffin shut. "I worked quite hard for it. It seems rude to pass it up."

"So rude," said Faith. "It's always best when we get what we deserve."

"Do you deserve the scholarship?" Devon asked.

Lia flinched. He couldn't be baiting her. Lia pulled a metal mechanical pencil from her pocket. She couldn't see them anymore.

Faith sniffed. "Of course I do. Just like you said. I worked quite hard for it."

Metal clicked against metal. Devon inhaled sharply.

"It might not even go to you," Devon said. "What are you going to do? Kill your way through every single high school in the district till you get it? They know about the emails. They can track your IP address."

Lia held still. Now Faith knew that he knew. That sound must have been the knife, but Faith didn't know it was fake. Devon was drawing all her plotting out from her and putting on a good show for the hidden camera. All Lia had to do was let it play out.

"My dad's a lawyer. I'll be fine. Lincoln High has the highest test scores in the district. Like some Park Hills student scored higher than me. Please." Faith laughed. Her phone clattered to the floor. "Pity Lia stole my phone. She's been so unpredictable this semester, don't you think? Probably the game and grief."

"That's very . . ." Devon hummed and took a deep breath. "Everyone worked hard for their scores. What makes you think you deserve it over us?"

"I'm not sure I deserve it more than you, but in a way, I do," Faith said. "Because I'm going to do more with it."

"Really?" he asked. "That's your justification?"

She still hadn't admitted to murder. Lia's limbs were so tense she feared she would never move again.

"You want to work in the ER," Faith said, fake gagging. "I want to save real lives."

"Yeah," Devon drawled, "murdering scholarship recipients for a miniscule chance to get their spot is going to be an excellent topic for your med school interviews. I can see it now. 'I wanted to be a surgeon so badly I killed a few of my classmates.' Really well done."

He hissed. Lia jerked, scared that Faith had hurt him.

"I'm fine," Devon said quickly, and Lia knew it was for her benefit. "You'll be a great surgeon but your bedside manner needs work."

But Lia's heart wouldn't calm.

"So what?" Faith slammed her hand against the benchtop. "I'm going to do real things. Important things. Who needs another vet? A communications major?" She snorted. "And Cassidy didn't even know what she wanted. At least Georgia had plans, even if they were bad ones."

"Had?" Devon asked. "What did you do?"

Lia swallowed. Her hands fisted at her sides, fingers trembling till she clenched them tight.

"What I tried to do to you, but neither of you cooperated. Well, this is fun, but I have a schedule to stick to," Faith said. "I assume Lia is here doing something stupid like recording me for later. Unless you have a gun, you should just come out."

Lia licked her lips and stood. She let her sleeve fall over her hand to cover the safety scissors. Faith waved at her with one hand, and her other held the knife to Devon's thigh. He glanced at her and shook his head. Lia shrugged.

"He'd survive that," Lia said.

Faith snorted. "You should've paid more attention in biology, but you being here makes this easier."

"Because I killed him?" Lia pointed to Devon.

Faith nodded. "Of course."

"Okay. Sure." Lia laid her hands flat against a desk, the scissors biting into her palm. Anger and fear flooded her veins. The knife wasn't real. She just had to remember that the knife wasn't real. "You've been banking on the scholarship for years, and if Abby, Cassidy, and Devon don't take them, one will fall to you, sure. But why Ben and Georgia?"

"Oh my God, you're impossible." Faith tilted her head back and shook it. "I had to kill Ben so that May would turn down her scholarship and to throw the cops off. It's not like he was doing anything. Georgia, same. Mostly. I think she scored higher than me."

She had finally said it.

"You think?" Devon spat.

"Why the messages?" Lia asked. "Why make me look like the killer?"

"Because you're jealous, obviously. You're an easy target. Poor little Lia Prince stuck in the shadow of her brother and jealous of all her smart friends ruining the one thing she has," she said. "And honestly, that journal makes you look like a killer anyway, scholarship angst or no."

"You really think you earned it?" Lia asked.

Faith lunged, pulling the knife away from Devon and pointing it at Lia's throat. "I am worth it. I'm a Franklin. I'm a legacy. I earned this, and then Abby came in and got it without even trying. Devon's fine—was fine—and all, but, I mean, but emergency medicine? Really? You might as well be a medical examiner for all the worth you'll be. You don't even know what you're doing! I'll be enough. I am."

Lia knew exactly what she was doing now.

"Why would I kill Devon?" Lia asked. "I can't figure that out."

"Of course you can't." Faith rolled her eyes. "You wanted to date. He didn't. He wanted to date. You didn't. Murder-suicide, blah blah blah. Maybe I'll make you leave a note."

The knife scraped up Lia's face to the corner of her eye. Even fake, that would do damage.

Devon grabbed Faith. "You don't—"

Faith spun. She slammed the knife into his chest, blade sinking all the way to the hilt, and blood splattered between them. Faith pulled back, the knife still in Devon's neck. He grasped the blade and fell from the chair. Blood pooled in the dirty cracks of the classroom floor.

Lia froze. Red freckled Faith's hands and face. Terror tangled around Lia's limbs, holding her in place, and Faith let out a disgusted sigh. She pulled a pile of paper towels toward herself. Devon lay still and silent.

The knife was fake. The knife was fake. The knife was fake.

"Don't tell me what to do," Faith muttered, wiping off her hands and walking to the other side of the bench. She pulled the knife from Devon with a wet squelch. "I hate that."

The blood was so bright that Lia's eyes burned.

"Okay, okay." Faith held out a hand to Lia. "Are you going to come here, or are you going to fight me?"

Lia pulled the scissors from her sleeve. Faith sighed and dove at her. The knife rammed into Lia's shoulder, pain blooming beneath it. Lia stumbled back, and Faith went with her. She ripped the knife up and stabbed Lia again. It hurt.

But not much.

Lia sliced the open scissors across her arm. Faith shrieked and fell back.

"How?" Faith asked, and she looked at the knife. A muscle in her jaw twitched.

She pressed the blade into her hand, and it sunk into the hilt. "You—"

Lia kicked her in the stomach and scrambled back. Faith crumbled, clutching her middle. The prop knife clattered to the floor. Blood leaked from the hilt.

"Me." Lia raised one hand slowly and pointed to Devon's phone planted high above eye level and staring down at all of them from the shelf. "Could you repeat it for the stream viewers in case someone joined after you confessed?"

Faith froze.

"Stream?" she whispered.

Hopefully a few were watching. They had to be. Everyone checked their phones after being cooped up in school all day.

"You're bluffing," Faith said, but whatever else she was going to say was lost beneath the sound of footsteps thundering up the steps to the stage.

Lia scrambled back and held up her scissors. Faith backed away, looking at Devon. He was still and bloody on the floor. Lia touched his face. He cracked open one eye and winked. The door flew open.

Faith wailed. A roar of voices spilled into the room. The door flew open behind them, and Lia didn't even look. Devon sat up slowly, groaning.

"What?" Lia asked. "How are—"

Devon only raised one bloody finger to Lia's lips. It tasted like corn syrup, glue, and too much food dye.

Lia gripped his shirt. "I thought you were dead." Lia wiped her face. "Why didn't you say anything?"

Devon hugged her close. "You got her to villain monologue. I couldn't interrupt that."

"I thought the knife failed," Lia said, fingers skimming where it had struck.

"Ow," he mumbled against her cheek. "Okay, wait, no. I'm not dead but ow. It just nicked me. There was still a squib in the hilt."

The fake blood, sweet and sickly, clumped against his skin. The blade, still metal, had pierced his skin. The squib must have stopped it from retreating all the way. He laid his cheek against her shoulder.

Nothing about this was funny, but relief swam over her and Lia laughed. Faith kept crying until the cops arrived and separated them all. The paramedics took Devon away despite his protests, and Lia waited at the edge of the crowd. Detective James wasn't there yet, but they took initial statements while it was all fresh.

The moment the cuffs clicked shut, Faith stopped crying. Her gaze slipped to Lia.

"Don't worry," Lia said. "You earned this."

"It's the one thing she did earn," a voice whispered near her ear. Devon was back, his arm bandaged.

"Maybe we should get you a real knife," Lia said, wrapping one arm around him. "Everyone says college is more brutal than high school."

CHAPTER 32

The cemetery where Abby was buried didn't allow dogs, so Lia brought pictures of dogs instead. The end of March had come and gone quickly, and Lia couldn't remember April, though she was pretty sure she hadn't napped through it. Grief and panic had made a blur of everything, smearing the edges of even last year's memories until it was all Before and After. The final day, though, was as clear as if Lia were still living it. She hadn't been able to go near the auditorium since. Georgia had been poisoned—Faith had laced her granola bar with something toxic—but miraculously, she hadn't died. Lia had heard that she was finally out of the hospital.

Lia had only returned to school four times since that day with Faith. All of them were mostly cruising till graduation. None of the teachers want to be *that* teacher and yell at someone for not working.

Apparently, the high school administration was fairly touchy about being known as Serial Killer High online, with competitive kids killing over grades. They had brought in extra counselors and therapists to work with the students, and they had agreed to let

Lia finish school with relaxed hours in class. Most of her work was handled at home or at Gem's. Gem had tried to tell the security guards what was happening in the drama room and hadn't been believed at all until a dozen seniors started sprinting toward it and the cops were called. Gem's parents hadn't been as kind to the front office as Lia's.

They probably would've believed Lia sooner.

"They finally stopped sending out those letters about cutting class," Lia said, giving Abby's shiny new headstone a sympathy pat. "I think the front office took about a month to catch up with what my counselor had arranged."

"Caught a murderer and didn't die," muttered Devon. "What more do they want from you?"

Lia reached over and nudged his leg. "Anyway, Faith's going to jail. For a long, long time."

Faith's parents had hired the best defense attorney in the state, and any time Lia saw them on the news, they were silent and stone-faced. They never looked at Faith. It was like she wasn't there at all. But Faith had found a new sort of attention in the dregs of the internet. Some people agreed with Faith and thought she had deserved the scholarship. They weren't kind in their comments about why.

Lia had deleted her social media accounts after that.

And she'd also accepted that the game was over. The Council never announced a winner—and somehow, she was okay with that. She and Gem and Devon had all won, really.

They were alive.

Carefully, she laid a new picture of Omelet, biodegradable and cleared by the cemetery's front office, next to the wilting flowers and mementos. "May adopted a dog. He's the wrinkliest pug, like

five years old already and breathes like a tornado, but she likes
him. He tried to eat Gem's socks."

"My favorite pair of socks," Gem added from somewhere behind Lia. "The little goblin." Lia knew Gem had spent a lot of
time recently at May's house, supporting her. It was going to take
a long time to accept everything that had happened.

Lia stood up and glanced back at Gem and Devon, who waited
a few steps behind her. Gem had returned to class. Devon hadn't
returned to school, and his parents had dared the office to say
anything. It was amazing what getting stabbed on school property
did for administrative red tape.

"Ready?" he asked. He had on a concert T-shirt and a pair of
athletic shorts. The mark on his arm was all but gone. You had to
look really close to see it. "We can walk if you're not."

"I have no good socks left," Gem whispered to him. "Don't
volunteer me to walk."

"I would carry you, but I got stabbed." He shrugged.

Gem snorted. "You didn't even need stitches."

"I'm ready," Lia said, and joined her friends. "Come on. No
carrying required."

"Are you sure you're ready to go?" Devon hooked one arm
through Lia's, the loose weight of his arm against hers as warm as
the sun peeking through the spring clouds above them. "It's not
like we have much to do. We can wait around."

"No, I'm good," Lia said. "I don't know if this is for me."

Her therapist had suggested talking to Abby, but like everyone
else, had underestimated Lia's hatred of explaining her own feelings, even to ghosts. Instead of apologizing, she had tried talking
about everything else this time. It still felt weird.

Her mom was trying, and her dad was attempting something

like parenthood now that the seriousness of the past few months was clear. Mark had even taken a week off to come visit her, and their parents hadn't said a word about him missing class for Lia. That was nice.

New but nice.

A month ago, Lia's mind had been fixed on May as the month her childhood would end and the world hit her full force. Every choice had felt important and every mistake like the end of the world. Then death had come barreling in with all the grace of an angry eighteen-year-old who thought they were owed the world.

But after all that had happened, for the first time in ages fear didn't constrict her chest or speed up her heart. It didn't even rear its head.

"Your parents haven't been on you as much now, right?" Gem asked.

Lia nodded. "Yeah, they have been treating me a lot better, but I don't know how long it will last," she said. "They're already iffy on letting me visit Devon next year."

"It's only three hours away!" Devon pulled them to a stop, his fingers curling gently around her arm. "You can confront a killer but not have a boyfriend?"

Lia laughed. "It's funny when you say it like that." She wasn't sure what would happen between her and Devon. Things changed. People changed. Maybe Lia and Devon wouldn't like who the other became in four years.

But for now, they were together. And they had caught a murderer and not died. A long-distance relationship and college seemed a lot less daunting after that.

They walked through the cemetery grounds, avoiding stepping on headstones. It was a quiet and peaceful place, with trees and stone benches and ornate shrubbery. It made Lia sad to think of Abby here, but as far as final resting places went, it was pretty nice.

"Yeah, I think they put up a fight just for show. I'm not keeping to that rule," Lia said. She kissed his cheek. "I'm allowed to visit Gem—that is, if you still want me."

Gem gave her a gentle push. "Please. You are welcome anytime. I'm bringing a sleeping bag for you so you'll always have a place to crash."

Lia wasn't going to college. Not yet, at least, her mom kept saying. After everything, Lia wanted a break. She had gotten a job at a café a town over where fewer people knew her face. If nothing else, working would give her more control over her life. Maybe that was why her parents hated her new plan.

Devon exhaled with a whistle. "Let's just hope no underclassmen get any ideas about how to get a free pass senior year."

Suddenly, the sound of three phones vibrating at the same time disrupted the stillness of the cemetery grounds.

Lia looked at Gem and Devon, pulling her phone out of her pocket. Gem and Devon took their phones out as well.

A new email notification scrolled across Lia's phone.

"Hunting season is open?" Gem asked, reading aloud.

Lia opened hers.

Hello, assassins.
Are you ready to finish your jobs? This email serves as the official notice that you have not completed the final round of Assassins and still fall under our command. Instructions will follow.
Happy hunting,
The Council

"They're not serious," Devon said, shaking his head incredulously. "Right?"

"I don't know." Gem swallowed and checked another message. Assassins had been officially banned. No one had dared to argue it. No one even wanted to. "It looks like other people besides us got this message, too, even the ones who withdrew ages ago."

A second email appeared in Lia's inbox. It had no subject and took up only two lines.

"Let's not worry about the game anymore," Lia said, shivering in her paper-thin cotton top. The game was in the past. Her future, whatever it was, lay in front of her.

Devon reached for her hand. "Cold?"

"Yeah." An unsettling feeling had formed in her stomach. She ran her hands over her bare arms, which were now covered with goose bumps. Lia deleted the second email and put her phone away. "Come on. Let's get away from here."

Lia Prince, you will miss your friends next year,
but you have bigger things to worry about.
This time, we won't let you ruin our fun.
But then again, murder is a necessity. Fun is optional.
The Council

ACKNOWLEDGMENTS

I am so thrilled to be a part of Underlined and Penguin Random House!

I owe a tremendous amount of thanks to Wendy Loggia, who is an amazing editor and was a dream to work with. Alison Romig and the entire Underlined team—thank you, thank you, thank you.

Thank you, Rachel Brooks, for being the best agent I could have ever asked for.

Brent, thank you for being a great husband and suffering through the trials of living with me while I'm on deadline.

And as always, thank all of you for reading *The Game*. Happy hunting.

Don't miss another thrilling
read from Underlined

FOUND

Aiden isn't watching the movie.

My skin grows warm as I realize he's not even pretending to watch the movie.

"You know, you were the one who picked this." I extend a finger toward my laptop. "What happened to all that 'I can't believe you've lived in New Jersey for nearly a year and you still haven't seen *Garden State*'?"

I barely get the words out before Aiden's hand fits to my jaw and he leans in to kiss me. It's a good kiss, the kind that makes my skin tingle and the whole world fade away until we're the only two people on the planet. His free hand slides around my waist, pulling me closer, and a light sigh escapes from me. I could get so lost in him if I let myself.

That thought abruptly brings reality back into focus, and I shimmy from Aiden's arms until we're awkwardly sitting beside each other again in the reading chair that's meant for only one person. This chair, my bed, and my thrift-shop desk and dresser make up the entirety of the furniture in my room—unless you count the boxes I never bothered to unpack.

Easygoing almost to a fault, Aiden lets me go without protest, raising a single eyebrow. "Did you hear your mom or something?"

I shake my head and shift to the cushioned armrest so we're no longer smooshed together. "She left barely an hour ago. That would be a new record for world's shortest first date, even for her." I want to check the window, though, and he knows it.

Aiden toys with a thread from the frayed knee of my jeans. There's an ease to the way he's touching me that screams boyfriend. I shiver involuntarily, which in turn makes me inch my leg away.

"Would it be so horrible if she knew about me?" he says. "I mean, we've technically already met." He glances over at the hiking boots next to my dresser, the ones he sold me and Mom four months ago, before she and I hiked the Smoky Mountains over the summer. I'd wanted to go to Disneyland, but she gets superanxious in big crowds, so she surprised me with a road trip and a secluded weeklong hike instead, which, I'll admit now, turned out kind of amazing. So did the cute REI sales associate who oh so casually slipped me his number while Mom was checking out mini stoves.

I gnaw my lip, trying to think of a way to say that, yes, it would be horrible if Mom knew about him, without actually having to say yes. I settle on "It's not you."

In response, Aiden gives me a slow nod. "Right."

"It's not." I reach for the hand he's drawn back. "It's not even her. It's me."

He lets out a humorless laugh. "Ashamed of me, huh? No, I get it. Guys who volunteer at animal shelters are generally dicks."

"No." I let my mouth curve in a smile. "But they do sometimes smell like cat pee."

A genuine laugh erupts from Aiden. "Seriously? I try to be really careful about that."

I lean forward to brush his cheek with a kiss, catching a hint of something crisp and foresty and definitely not at all like cat pee. When I start to stand, Aiden tugs me back.

"Then what?" His voice is as gentle as his touch. "'Cause I keep expecting you to just ghost me one of these days, and I'm fully ready to admit how much that would suck." His hand slips over mine. "I like you, Katelyn. I'm fine if it's more than you like me, but tell me I'm not wasting my time here."

Every bit of the humor that initially attracted me to Aiden is gone. We've always kept things light and fun. Now he looks like my next words have all the power in the world to elate or crush him.

And I will crush him. Not intentionally, and probably not without crushing myself a bit in the process, but it's going to happen. Not because Aiden is a bad guy—I think the fact that he's in my bedroom despite all Mom's rules speaks for itself. As does the fact that he made a cute Rapunzel joke instead of complaining when I told him he'd have to climb the drainpipe and sneak into my bedroom if he wanted to see me. I couldn't risk letting him use the front entrance like a normal person (I wouldn't put it past Mom to rig the door with some kind of undetectable sign to check if it's been opened when she leaves me home alone).

I should probably explain about my mom.

She's amazing and funny—but nearly every hour of the day she's terrified out of her mind that something terrible is going to happen to me. I think it has to do with how she grew up. She's never been exactly forthcoming about her past, but I do know that her mom dropped her on the doorstep of her unsuspecting father's trailer when she was three, never to be seen again, and that the height of her dad's parenting skills was remembering to feed her most of the time. He died shortly before I was born, so I've never met him, but given my mom's lack of parental supervision growing up, it seems like she swung really far the other way with me.

Until a few years ago, the only time I was allowed on the computer was for school—home school, that is. And I think it was more my mom's fear of algebra than any of my pleading that finally made her relent and allow me to go to public school. Though, to be fair, it might also have been the hunger strike I enacted.

It took me a little longer to convince her to let me get a cell phone, which I finally accomplished by printing out news stories at school about kids who got kidnapped and saved themselves by calling for help. Were some of them stories I wrote myself using mock-up layouts I found online? Maybe. But sometimes my mom needs that extra push to rein in the superparanoid would-keep-me-in-a-bubble-forever mentality that defines her as a parent.

I've learned that the best way to get what I want is to either convince her I'm in more danger if she doesn't listen to my suggestions (e.g., public school, a cell phone) or just keep a few harmless details from her (e.g., Aiden).

Most days, I think she knows I cut corners when it comes to her rules, but I like to think she's the teeniest bit proud of me when I figure out how to get around one. I'm not stupid enough to flaunt Aiden in front of her, though, which is why I practically shove him off the chair when I hear the front door open downstairs.

She did break her record. It isn't even nine o'clock yet.

"Katelyn?"

"In my room!" I call, jumping up and pushing Aiden toward the window.

"Is this my answer?" There's a teasing quality to his voice that I can appreciate only because he has the good sense to whisper.

"Know what happened to the last guy my mom found in my room?"

"He got invited to dinner?"

"He got a face full of pepper spray." All because he was trying to decorate my room to invite me to a dance. Poor guy. And poor me, since Mom and I ended up moving right after—Mom says the two are unrelated, but I doubt it.

She calls it wanderlust, but I'm not sure that's what it is. She'll be fine one day, and the next I'll come home from school to find that she's quit her job and already has half our belongings in boxes—hence the unpacked ones stacked in my room. We're closing in on a year in our current duplex, and I'm hoping to make it through graduation here, if nothing else. But that means getting Mom to make some ties in Bridgeton so she won't want to leave the next time she gets an itch.

My greatest triumph of the past year was getting her to agree to start dating, something she hasn't done since my dad died, despite the frequent offers she gets. She had me when she was only nineteen, so she's still young and looks amazing—also thanks to the fact that we run together every morning. She has stunning green eyes and thick auburn hair that reaches halfway down her back. My eyes and hair are the same color as hers but not nearly as striking. The main difference between us is that my skin is more olive than her fair, sunburn-prone complexion, a gift from a man I barely remember.

Based on the way she still tears up on the rare occasions I get her to talk about my dad, I'm not expecting her to fall madly in love with one of the guys she dates, but a little flirting and fun would be good for her. And any reason to stay in one place long enough for it to feel like home is good enough for me.

If she found Aiden in my room, she'd have a moving truck in our driveway before he even made it out the window.

I push him again. "You have to go."

"Meet me tomorrow."

"I—" I start to object, since I have no idea how I'll slip away from Mom, but he looks perfectly content—eager, even—to get caught. "Fine."

"Promise?"

I almost grit my teeth, but I remember that he's still waiting for my answer about whether he's wasting his time with me. I know what I want the answer to be, but hearing Mom's footsteps on the stairs, I give Aiden one last shove. "I promise." He climbs out the window, only to dart back in the second I start to turn away—to kiss me one more time.

"Go!" I hiss, trying not to smile. I don't breathe again until he clears the frame so I can close the window and yank the curtain shut.